I Had Never Heard a City Cry Before

by Mike Gibb

Cover artwork by David Stout of Sketchpad

First published by Hame Press on 6 July 2023 with the generous support of the Doric Board.

This book is dedicated to the memory of the 229 victims of the Piper Alpha oilfield disaster; the 167 who died and the 62 who survived.

"An honest man's the noblest work of God"
Alexander Pope.

Best Wishes.

BY THE SAME WRITER

Plays & Musical Plays

A Land Fit for Heroes
Mother of All the Peoples
Five Pound & Twa Bairns
Sunday Mornings on Dundee Law
Clarinda
Red Harlaw
Aberdeen's Forgotten Diva
Outlander the Musical
Children of the Sea
Lest We Forget
Doorways in Drumorty
Giacomo & Glover
Walking Down the Halbeath Road

Books

It's A Dawgs Life
Waiting For the Master
Ask Anna
How to Train Your Owner
Anna's Adventures in Wonderland
When Angus Met Donny
Sammy the Tammy (The Mystery of the Missing Mascot)
The Name's Sammy, Sammy the Tammy
Drumorty Revisited
Forgotten Heroines of the North East
A Stepping Stone to Stardom
Heroes of the Halbeath Road
Forgotten Heroes of the North East

PROLOGUE

In 1969 employees of Philips Petroleum were operating in a sector of the North Sea allocated by the British Government for oil exploration. The company had already dug more than 30 holes with no success and were all for giving up and admitting failure when on 23 June they decided to give it one last try. They struck gold or in this case black gold.
The following day the news appeared on the front page of the Press & Journal, the local Aberdeen morning paper, although few people who read the article would have appreciated the significance of the find or how much it would change the city. For those involved in the oil industry, however, it was an event of great significance and the word on the lips of every CEO of every oil company worldwide was 'Bonanza' as they headed for a place that until then they hadn't even know existed. Before long the rather staid folk in the Granite City had to get used to the sight of men strutting down Union Street wearing Stetson hats and cowboy boots.
Dr. Armand Hammer, the CEO of Occidental, was not a man who wanted to turn up late to any party and his company obtained the rights to drill in oil fields, which later became known as Piper and Claymore, a hundred and thirty miles off the coast of the Orkney Islands. Having secured the rights the company were then faced with twin tasks, to find a base for an onshore terminal to receive the oil and to build platforms to extract it.

The former was achieved after considerable scouting of the area when the small island of Flotta south-west of the Orkney Mainland was identified and work in building an oil terminal began, one that was subsequently linked to offshore platforms by an undersea pipeline. Around the same time the task of constructing the first of the platforms was entrusted to McDermott's yard at Ardersier on the Moray Firth east of Inverness.

The platform gained the nickname of the 'Monster' because of its size; it was 495 ft tall. Work began in autumn 1973 with the platform due for completion by June 1974. Due to a dispute between two of the Unions, which resulted in a strike, completion was delayed and the chance to move the massive structure in summer when the weather was more benign was lost. It was in fact a year later before that task could be carried out and Hammer was so annoyed by the situation that the rig destined to be built for the adjacent Claymore field was subsequently constructed in Cherbourg in France.

Towed by huge barges the 'Monster' was positioned in the North Sea where it acquired a new name, Piper Alpha. The first oil from that platform began to flow on 27 December 1976 although the official opening was on 11 January the following year, an event attended by a host of investors from far and near, many arriving at the small Kirkwall Airport by private jet.

By 1979 the platform was working at maximum capacity and on one day in that year it yielded up 317,000 barrels of oil, the most produced by any platform anywhere in the world on a single day. At that time the oil price was around $40 per

barrel meaning that the value of the oil extracted on that one day was some 12 million dollars.
While never achieving that again Piper Alpha continued to produce high levels of oil some 365 days a year for the next decade. Right up until 10.00 pm on the night of Wednesday 6 July 1988.

CHAPTER ONE

Kenny Mutch loved to live by the sea. Indeed, until he turned eighteen and headed off to college in Aberdeen, he had never had any desire to leave Peterhead where he was born and raised, happy to live within the warm embrace of the Blue Toon. Although warm embrace may not be the most appropriate epithet for a town perched in a remote corner of north-east Scotland, regularly peering though the haar at the cold grey North Sea.

As far as Kenny was concerned Peterhead had everything he could possibly want. A lot of shops, its own cinema, the Playhouse on Queen Street, even its own prison. It also allowed him to vigorously pursue his main hobby.

Kenny could be described as a seafaring version of the train spotter. From an early age Kenny was a regular sight at Peterhead harbour where he would sit for hours on end armed with a notebook, a pen, chopped pork sandwiches, a bottle of Sang's Lemonade and a pair of Carl Zeiss German World War II binoculars.

The binoculars were one of his most prized possessions and had been given to him by his Granddad McKay who had brought them home from the war. What was constant about the oft related story of how Sandy McKay came to acquire the binoculars was that it always involved him shooting 'krauts', as his Granddad insisted on calling them. What varied, in direct correlation to the number of times he poured from the ever present bottle of the Famous Grouse into his waiting glass, were the number of enemy soldiers he sent to an early grave. It was only after the old man had passed that Kenny's Mum revealed that her Dad had in fact found the binoculars lying at the side of the road when he was marching through Belgium and that no German soldiers were harmed in acquiring them.

Whatever their provenance Kenny loved them. Not only could he spot vessels heading towards the harbour long before they berthed but it made him hugely popular with many of his school pals who loved to gather in his room and focus them on the Wendy Morrison's bedroom window across the street.

Now most people who stayed in that part of the country would be able to work out that a trawler arriving with identification letters such as FR would be from Fraserburgh or BCK from Buckie. But how many could tell that LT meant the vessel had sailed from Lowestoft or that SSS was from the exotic location of South Shields? Kenny Mutch could as well as recognising boats from many other obscure places.

What Kenny couldn't tell you with any degree of accuracy was when the change began as it was in truth gradual. But slowly he became aware that amongst the flotilla of fishing boats were these strange flat vessels, usually painted in bright colours like yellow or orange or red. They were, of course, supply boats carrying a wide variety of goods to the oil platforms and rigs that had sprung up in the North Sea, all of them sadly positioned so far over the horizon that they couldn't be seen even with the aid of his Granddad's powerful binoculars.

Kenny came from a seafaring family. His Granddad Mutch was the owner and skipper of a trawler, the *Buchan Rose*, while his Dad, George, was the first mate. Although the subject was never discussed it was assumed that when Kenny left school he would join them for a life on the ocean wave. But then one fateful day everything suddenly changed. For them all.

Kenny's father would always blame himself for what happened despite the fact that everyone would tell him that it was an accident, plain and simple. Whenever that was said his George would simply nod his head, pretending to agree, while remaining unconvinced and wracked with guilt.

The simple fact was that if anyone was to blame it was Kenny's Granddad who carelessly took a short cut from one side of the deck to the other as the crew were tossing a seine net into the sea. The man himself would lecture new crew members never to do just that but sadly forgot his own cardinal rule. On that fateful day one of his boots caught in the mesh and he was dragged overboard by the weight of the net. The horrified crew reacted immediately, reversing the winch in the vain hope that the net would bring back the skipper with it. Sadly it didn't.

The boat spent several hours going around in every decreasing circles trying to find the man while fully aware that it was a futile exercise; no one could survive more than fifteen minutes in the icy winter waters of the North Sea.

On the night after a memorial service for his Grandfather had been held in St Andrews Church Kenny sat down at the kitchen table with his Dad for a man to man talk. George spoke at length of how he had no intention of interfering in the young lad's life and whatever he decided to do after he left school was entirely up to Kenny and nobody else. Just as long as he didn't go to sea. Neither he nor his wife wanted to spend the rest of their days worrying if the boy would return safely each and every time he sailed out of the harbour.

George probably thought that he would have a battle on his hands to convince the teenager and was surprised, and delighted, when the lad readily agreed. Although he never let on to his parents Kenny had been dreading the day he would have to become a trawler man. He had been on his Granddad's boat many times but only when it was tied up at the quayside and even then the gentle swaying made him feel sick and had no wish to ever leave the safety of the harbour.

Having witnessed what had happened to his father George Mutch was a broken man. He sold the boat and never set foot on any vessel again. He began work at the Consolidated Pneumatic Tool Company in Fraserburgh until he tired of the commuting and settled for a job in the local ironmongers where he remained until he died prematurely aged 47.

Kenny and his Dad had been really close and the lad desperately missed the father figure in his life. In an effort to fill the gap Kenny's mother, Jean, had asked her brother Stan to step in and take the boy under his wing and while Kenny went along with it and liked his Uncle Stan it wasn't the same. When on a Saturday Stan suggested taking Kenny into Aberdeen to the pictures or to Pittodrie for the football Kenny would go but only if he couldn't think up a valid excuse to

avoid it. His mother quickly pointed out that *I'm going to my Grunnies* didn't come under the heading of 'valid excuse'.
Mind you there was one day in his mid teens when he jumped at the chance to go out with Uncle Stan and Cousin Peter; the Scottish League Cup Final was being played at Hampden in Glasgow and the date of 6 November 1976 would be etched in his brain from that day forward. Until that morning Kenny had never been further south than Aberdeen, never in any football stadium but Pittodrie. But then he suddenly found himself staring out of the car window at places with mysterious sounding names like Laurencekirk and Auchterarder before arriving in the metropolis itself.
For the first ten minutes inside Hampden Park he sat in his seat in the main stand and just stared at the crowd as, not surprisingly, he had never seen seventy thousand people in one place before. It was awesome. For Kenny, oblivious to the heavy rain, it was the perfect day as he watched the lads in red and white being totally outplayed by their Celtic counterparts but yet somehow emerging as victors and taking the old trophy north with them.
From that day forth he was a Dons fan. He didn't often get to see them play, not until he was much older anyway, but listened intently to the radio on a Saturday to see how they were performing before updating his *Roy of the Rovers* wall chart with its cardboard pegs in clubs' names and colours to reflect Aberdeen's latest league position.

But while the conversation with his Dad had cemented what Kenny was not going to do with his life it left him quite unaware of what the future would hold for him. Speak to most school teachers about past pupils and they will probably only remember those in two categories – the ones who excelled and the ones who caused trouble. Kenny Mutch fell into neither grouping. If you had asked any teacher at Peterhead Academy what they remember of Kenny Mutch all, with one exception, would probably have answered 'who'?.

Kenny could be described as an average student, not doing brilliantly in any subject but equally never disastrously. The only subjects that contravened that rule were Art, where he shone, and French, the ability to say little more than bonjour and au revoir being insufficient to earn him an 'O' level pass.

His love of art came from his maternal grandmother who was an enthusiastic and fairly decent artist turning out pleasant watercolours which adorned every wall of every room of her small cottage in Boddam. She encouraged Kenny and much to his delight and surprise he found that he had a natural talent for drawing. The surprise element emanated from the fact that until he discovered that flair he had never excelled at anything, his lack of ability at a variety of sports proving a major disappointment to his father who had a drawer full of medals earned on the junior football field.

Kenny was therefore delighted when the art teacher at Peterhead Academy, Trevor Wainwright, took him under his wing. Mr Wainwright was somewhat different to most of the other teachers at the Academy both in attitude, treating his pupils with respect, and in appearance. While many of his male counterparts dressed in clothes rescued from the sale rail at the local House of Fraser, purchased because of price and not because they fitted, Mr. Wainwright would arrive wearing a variety of linen and corduroy jackets, slacks that looked made to measure and a selection of waistcoats in a wide variety of vivid colours which on someone less stylish would have looked garish. With his neatly trimmed light brown hair and goatee beard it was hardly surprising that many teenage girls happily trooped along to his class not to study but merely to stare in awe at the teacher.

It was in his second year at the Academy that this teacher identified Kenny's talent and cultivated it. With his support and guidance Kenny sailed through his 'O' level in the subject and, with his mother's persuasion to stay on at school, subsequently gained the Higher grade. At that stage Mr. Wainwright suggested that Kenny apply for a place at Gray's School of Art in Aberdeen and more to please his mentor than anything else he did so but without telling another soul what he had done. He had two reasons for his secrecy. If, as he suspected, he was turned down he wouldn't appear a failure in the eyes of family and friends. Alternatively, in the unlikely event that he did secure entry, he wouldn't have to mention it to anyone as he had no intention of going.

Kenny had two younger siblings, his brother Brian and the baby of the family, Shirley. As a consequence when his father died so young Kenny stepped up to the plate to become the man of the house. To ensure that he would not be in anyway a financial drain on his mother he got a job delivering the Press & Journal six mornings a week before heading for school and worked in the newsagents on a Sunday. As a result of enjoying a share of the money from the sale of the *Buchan*

Rose Jean Mutch was left, in Peterhead parlance, 'comfortably aff'. At the same time Kenny didn't want his mother to have to divert any of her finite income in putting him through Art College.

He had already worked out a strategy for when the response to his application arrived from the School of Art. If, as he suspected he was rejected he would feign disappointment to Mr Wainwright and get on with his life. If he was accepted he would feign disappointment to Mr Wainwright, citing his mother's situation as a poor widowed women who needed her son's emotional and financial support, and get on with his life. Scotland's national bard penned the famous lines 'the best laid schemes of mice and men, gang aft a-gley' and Kenny could certainly testify to the accuracy of that statement. Returning home from the Academy one afternoon he noticed auld Miss Sinclair staring out of the window of the neighbouring house. Now that in itself wasn't unusual; if she hadn't been there that would have been strange as Miss Sinclair lived on her own except for a bad tempered Tabby cat called Peter and, riddled with arthritis, seldom left her home, spending her days peering out of her sitting room window at the comings and goings on Maiden Street. What was different that afternoon is that the generally solemn Miss Sinclair was beaming like a cat, of the Cheshire not Tabby variety, and giving the two thumbs up sign to Kenny.

Her actions rather confused him but he put it down to his mother's suggestion that Miss Sinclair was sometimes 'a bittie confused'. However, once he reached home he realised that her behaviour had nothing to do with the old lady's mental health as all was revealed. His normally undemonstrative mother rushed to greet him, smothering him in a bear hug. Behind her stood his sister with a smirk on her face, holding a letter, a letter that clearly bore the heading 'Gray's School of Art'. It appeared that her sister had been sent home early from her primary school because she wasn't feeling well, a fairly regular occurrence in her case. Kenny considered his sister to be a hypochondriac who, having found out what the word virus meant, developed one with repetitive regularity.

She had found the letter when she arrived at the house and opened it despite the fact that it was clearly addressed to Mr. Kenneth Mutch and not Miss Shirley Mutch, an easy mistake to make since the words Kenneth and Shirley were so similar. She couldn't wait for her mother to appear so she could be first on the block to impart the news.

Despite the fact that there was less than an hour between her arrival at the family home and that of her son, Jean had managed to spread the word not only to old Miss Sinclair but to her own sister Rhona, her cousin Brenda, Mr. Ahmed at the corner shop and Old Uncle Tom Cobley and all.

A long evening of discussion ensued with Kenny trying to convince his mother that going to College wasn't a good idea, not in their financial situation, although all through those twilight hours Kenny knew that he was facing a losing battle. Having told so many people there was no way that his mother was going to reveal that she had got it wrong and hell would freeze over before she would face Cousin Brenda with such a climb down. For years she had been faced with Brenda crowing about her darling boy Malcolm who was a pupil at

Robert Gordon's College in Aberdeen and now at last Jean had one up on her. After all, acceptance at a prestigious art college was surely several rungs about a place at a fee paying school especially when the hefty fees were paid for by the boy's father from the proceeds of his business which Jean, without any proof, always described as 'dodgy'.

Resigned to his fate Kenny began to research the Art school and was shocked to discover that it was situated in the Garthdee area on the south side of Aberdeen which totally scuppered his hope that he could commute daily from Peterhead. As a result he had no option but to reluctantly apply for accommodation in halls of residence where he discovered that he would be sharing with three other guys. Two of them were from Tunbridge Wells and had clearly passed numerous similar educational establishments on their way north, choosing this far flung northern outcrop for no other reason than to get as far away from their homes and their parents as possible. The other member of the threesome was local, hailing from a rather posh part of Aberdeen, and Kenny quickly discovered that conversing with all of them was far from easy as they had difficulty in understanding his broad Aberdeenshire accent, littered with words of Doric origins.

Kenny's mother lived by the maxim that cleanliness was next to Godliness and that tidiness wasn't far behind. Kenny was therefore horrified that none of his fellow students ever washed an item of crockery and allowed dishes to pile up in the sink only occasionally swilling a plate or a cup in cold water when not a single clean remained. Twice during his first couple of weeks he spent an hour doing all the dishes and genuinely tidying the place in the hope that the others would get the hint and follow his example. When that didn't materialise Kenny headed for the nearby Asda superstore where he bought his own crockery and cutlery which he would wash after use and keep in his own bedroom.

It was while he was in Asda that he spotted a 'Staff Wanted' notice and decided to apply. He needed to find employment of some sort to pay for his keep but was dismayed to find that the store were looking for 'Ambient Replenishment Assistants' and concluded that he wouldn't be qualified for such a position. It was only when he was discussing it with a fellow student that it was explained to him that it was no more than a fancy name for a shelf stacker. And so he applied and got the job, working five evenings a week and every Saturday thereby allowing him to attend all classes and return home to Peterhead every Sunday to accompany his Mother to Church. The work was repetitive and boring but paid reasonably well and also allowed him to converse with people that didn't speak with a Kent or Rubislaw Den accent and with whom he could have a good blether. It was one day while he was working with a fellow young guy stacking a shelf with tins of Heinz baked beans that the first roots of a friendship were established, one that would dramatically affect his life. His fellow ambient replenishment assistant was a lad by the name of Steven Grant.

CHAPTER TWO

Martin Grant and Eveyln Watson arrived as twelve year olds at Aberdeen Academy, in the heart of the city, on the same day and with the same sense of trepidation, decked out in pristine new bottle green blazers. Having spent their early school years cosseted at Skene Square and Mile End Primaries respectively they knew that life in the Academy, with its reputation for strict discipline, would be rather different. And so it proved although as dedicated and well behaved students it caused neither of them any major problem or concern and they sailed effortlessly through their secondary school years.

For the first couple of those Martin and Evelyn were little more than nodding acquaintances as boys and girls largely kept themselves to groups of the same sex. However by the third year as hormones kicked in things began to change and they found a mutual attraction. And that was that. For the remainder of their time at the Academy they were an 'item', both leaving together with top grades sufficient to get them into Aberdeen University to study medicine. Everyone was convinced that they would be a married couple in no time at all but being sensible and disciplined people they waited six years before tying the knot to ensure that planning a wedding and all that entailed didn't interfere with their studies.

Their plans were successful and by the time they had both turned thirty Martin was a Consultant at Aberdeen Royal Infirmary and Evelyn a G.P. at a well known local medical group. As a result the couple were sufficiently wealthy to buy the house of their dreams. It was a majestic, granite, semi-detached property, three stories in height, on the prestigious thoroughfare of King's Gate. It provided them with considerably more accommodation than they needed in the form of three public rooms and five bedrooms and the couple were immensely proud of it. In his later years Steven, just to annoy his parents, would tell people he lived in a semi.

Evelyn was almost a week short of her thirty fifth birthday when Steven arrived on the scene and four weeks later she was back at work. It became clear that neither her nor her husband were willing to give up their respective vocations to look after the boy who was entrusted to a nanny. With his mother working long hours and his Dad supplementing his already lucrative income with what Steven liked to call 'homers' at the private St. John's Hospital, he saw little of his parents.

One attraction of living in such a huge house was that from an early age Steven could hide away in a bedroom on the top floor only meeting up with his parents at meal times. Even then he was never invited to any of the countless dinner parties his parent's hosted with remarkable regularity and would have to eat in the kitchen with his nanny before the glitterati of the Aberdeen medical scene arrived.

Steven had a few good pals to play with and as a result when the time came for him to go to school he was looking forward to attending Mile End Primary with his friends. Unfortunately his mother and father had other plans for him.

There was no family discussion on the subject and the first Steven knew that he had been enrolled at Robert Gordon's, the city's foremost fee paying establishment for boys, was when he was dragged down to the Esslemont & MacIntosh's department store to be measured for his school uniform. A month later he suddenly found himself being escorted right into the centre of Aberdeen by his nanny and deposited in what appeared, to a small boy anyway, to be an enormous austere establishment.

He was terrified especially as there wasn't a boy that he knew in the whole school with the sole exception of Trevor who lived nearby but who no one ever spoke to because they thought he was a wimp who would never play with the rest of them in the woods on Woodhill Road, preferring to stay at home with his stamp collection.

Steven hated having to wear a fancy uniform. He hated all the school rules. He hated the teachers who would shout at you for the slightest infringement of those rules. Basically he hated everything about the school.

Throughout his first year he complained bitterly about it to his mother, who he thought might be more sympathetic than his father, and even resorted to tears in the hope that it might encourage her to move him to Mile End where all his pals seemed to be having a whale of a time. It didn't work and as a five year old really has no say in anything at all Steven had no option but go back the next year. And the one after.

Steven was also horrified to discover that football, a game that he was pretty decent at, wasn't tolerated at Gordon's where everyone was expected to participate in 'rugger'. Steven quickly became convinced that rugby was a game that involved no skill just brute force and had been devised by bullies to be played by bullies and he detested games afternoons even more than days in classrooms.

By the time he had completed seven miserable years Steven was due to move up to the senior school; he had, however, already decided that there was no way he was going to spend another five or six years in that place or even another five minutes for that matter. Discussions on the subject were lengthy and heated but eventually both of his parents realised that they were no longer faced with a child but with a strong willed lad on the verge of becoming a teenager and reluctantly they had no option but to wave the white flag. They were in the catchment area for Aberdeen Grammar School which had a decent reputation so they accepted that Steven could go there.

But having got his parents on the run Steven was far from finished and threw a spanner in the works by insisting he followed in the footsteps of Mater and Pater who constantly recalled with great fondness their time at Aberdeen Academy.

They had such affection for that place that they were staunch supporters of the former pupils' club regularly attending gatherings with ex-school pals.

The only problem was that, much to their disgust, their beloved Academy had been turned into a shopping centre, of all things, and the uniform and the school motto and much more that they held so dear had been transferred to Hazlehead Academy which had a catchment area of Summerhill and even, much to their horror, the council estates of

Sheddocksley. Seated around a table in what his parent insisted on calling the drawing room, they tried to persuade Steven to think again totally ignorant of the fact that the only reason that Steven wanted to go there was because they didn't. It proved difficult for them to object, however, when the boy had been raised on a diet of how wonderful their Academy school days had been and eventually they were forced to agree to his decision.

Steven loved it. After seven years at the staid Robert Gordon's, Hazlehead Academy had edginess to it largely due to the influx of pupils from the schemes that his parents didn't want him to mix with. His first year was fairly tame as he found his feet but by year two he accompanied some of the more audacious fellow students in regular visits to the rector's room and not for the purpose of being showered with accolades. In most cases Steven had been little more than a bit player in the merry japes of others except for one occasion which earned him legendary status amongst an element of the other pupils. The school motto was 'Ad altiora tendo' which translated from the Latin meant 'I strive for higher thing' which Steven misinterpreted in an infamous incident involving a fifth year girl.

His parents, summoned to the school with increasing and depressing regularity, became conditioned to the fact that their one and only offspring was not going to follow them along the path of taking the Hippocratic oath and indeed they could only hope that the path he did follow didn't lead to Aberdeen Sherriff Court. With grades little more than average any possibility of University was shelved and aged sixteen an ecstatic Steven took his first steps into the post-scholastic world.

Speaking to anyone about his childhood Steven would regularly complain about his lot while conveniently omitting to mention the good times. And there were good times, especially the holidays. He was ten years old when his Mum and Dad sat him down at the table for what he assumed would be the latest lecture about his behaviour. But no, this was to inform him that they had just finished planning the summer holiday and that both of them had arranged for three weeks off work. When they told him where they intended going he initially assumed that he had misheard before it eventually dawned on him that they did really mean 'New York'. Most of the kids in his class ended up in a caravan at Oban or a bed and breakfast in Blackpool and he couldn't wait to get back to school the next day to spread the news.

But New York proved to be only the beginning of that adventure. Suddenly his rather sedate father seemed to emerge like a butterfly from a chrysalis as he hired a fancy Camero sports car and drove them south down the I-95 all the way to Florida. Every stop was at a motel with an outdoor swimming pool, every meal was eaten in a burger joint or somewhere selling delicious spare ribs in BBQ sauce. And when they got to the Sunshine State they then headed for Disney's Magic Kingdom.

Steven had supposed that it would be a one off, a holiday of a lifetime, but within weeks of returning his Dad had the Rand McNally U.S. map book out as he began planning an itinerary for the next summer. And that proved to be the annual format until the summer that Steven left school and declared that he would rather stay at home. But looking back Steven had to admit that those holidays had left him with some wonderful memories. As a film buff from an early age he couldn't believe he could actually look up at the famous Hollywood sign or drive past all the big movie studios. Even more exciting to him was a visit to a real cowboy town like Durango or to drive past Monument Valley where so many Western movies had been filmed.

The only down side to those holidays was the fact that they had to return home after three glorious weeks and suddenly, as if some 2nd assistant cameraman had brought down the clapperboard, the scene changed with his parents instantly returning to their busy lives and Steven to his forlorn garret.

The first few months after leaving school were idyllic for Steven. He had the house to himself and could lie in bed until lunchtime with no one to shout at him to get up. The allowance he received from his darling parents was sufficient to keep him in beer and records and fags; he was banned from smoking in the house but that didn't stop him as he would hang out of the top floor window and let the evidence drift off in the breeze. Eventually, however, his parents wearied of subsidising his hedonistic lifestyle and his presence was requested in the drawing room for another of the nights of the round table where it was made clear that unless he gained some meaningful employment no further cash would be heading his way.

Now he wasn't too concerned about beer supplies being discontinued. After all he was only sixteen and as such shouldn't legally have been touching the stuff. Cigarettes were also not a major problem. He had only taken up smoking because all the other members of the group he hung around with at school were doing it and Steven really didn't like the taste.

But cutting off his access to records was a serious issue. From the moment he opened his eyes in the morning until he went off to the land of nod at night, music emanated from his room. Being closeted away at the top of the house and with thick stone walls separating them from the neighbours, noise pollution wasn't a major issue although from time to time a complaint came from downstairs when he revisited the punk era. Shelves in his bedroom accommodated his collection of vinyl records while the walls were decorated with the sleeves of his very favourite albums.

He was a regular visitor to One Up Records where he was always greeted with a smile and had the chance to discuss music with like minded aficionados. Indeed one of the few reasons he would rise before lunchtime was if a new album by The Who or the Stones or a dozen other groups was being released that day. The thought that he wouldn't be able to buy new records as soon as they appeared on the scene filled him with such horror that reluctantly he went in search of gainful employment.

The joint problems he encountered were that he wasn't trained for any job and that he was allergic to hard work. He daily scanned the local evening newspaper to see if there was

anything that might suit him but realised that they nearly all had one major disadvantage; starting time was usually long before he normally surfaced. But then up popped a job at Asda where he wouldn't have to report for duty until afternoon and where he would be set free in time to head for one of the city centre nightclubs which didn't normally fill up and warm up until late in the day. Perfect.
He applied and was accepted as the recruitment procedure for someone to stack toilet rolls and the like wasn't too demanding and he found himself working for the first time in his life alongside a guy of similar age.

Oh hello, you're surely new.
Yes first day.
Oh weel you'll be gled o' the experience I've built up.
Have you worked here long?
Aye, nearly twa wiks! I'm an expert shelf stacker by now.
Is this your full time job?
No. I'm a student at the College up the road.
What are you studying?
Art.
Oh so you must be pretty good at drawing to get in there.
Weel I thoucht I wis 'til I arrived. Nae so sure now. Some o' them there are brilliant. Are you at Uni as weel?
No.
So fit dae you dae?
This. And only this.
But you must hae somethin' in mind as a career?

Yes, of course. I'm studying to become a senior ambient replenishment assistant!
Seriously, fit are you plans?
Truthfully I don't have a clue. The only thing I really fancy being is a DJ but Mummy and Daddy aren't impressed by that idea.
So are you a music fan?
Big music fan. Love the idea of getting paid for playing records that I like. But until that happens, if it does, I guess I'll just have to carry on putting one tin of beans on top of another. By the way, I'm Steven.
Kenny. I'm fae Peterheid.
I never would have guessed!

Steven Grant and Kenny Mutch soon became inseparable despite being somewhat like the odd couple. Kenny was of medium height, medium build and medium good looks. Steven on the other hand was tall and well built despite the fact that the only exercise he ever enjoyed involved the lifting of pints of lager. He also had a mop of unruly blonde hair and many a young girl would give him more than a second glance when passing him in the street. But it was more than physically they differed. The two lads had clearly come from very different backgrounds.

CHAPTER THREE

With difficulty Kenny and Steven managed to force their way through the street door into the communal vestibule of the tenement building on Holburn Street and once they had achieved that feat discovered that the impediment to gaining entry was an enormous heap of items of accumulated junk mail behind the door with a substantial preponderance of two-for-one pizza offers.

It was at that point that he concluded that the building was no doubt occupied by students from his own college and RGU. To Kenny it would surely have been easier to spend a few moments picking up the leaflets and dumping them in the bin rather than having to squeeze in and out of the building on a daily basis but clearly other potential captains of industry and the like didn't think that way.

Once the lads had manoeuvred their way into the tenement they made their way up a dingy and grubby staircase to a top floor two room flat. The words that instantly came to Kenny's mind when he saw it were those much beloved by estate agents 'in need of some modernisation'. However, it did have two great advantages – it was in walking distance of Gray's School of Art and the Asda Superstore and it was cheap and by pooling their meagre earnings they could afford the rental. Just.

They would have liked a place with two bedrooms but had to settle for what they could afford and worked out a rota for nights in the bedroom or on the sofa bed in the lounge, a schedule which they adhered to rigidly. Well unless they had a sudden and unexpected house guest of the female variety at which point a compromise was quickly worked out. But the restrictions of the flat were more than compensated for by the chance to get away from their current accommodation.

His folks seldom bothered him, leaving Steven to wonder how many days it would be after he had left before they realised he had actually gone. At the same time he felt that the time had come to spread his wings. Kenny was even more desperate for a change of scene. Despite the fact it was over six months since he had moved into the halls of residence he was no closer to calling any of his fellow flat mates 'friend' and indeed the other three seemed to have established a small clique that didn't include him. He was also weary of their untidiness and other disgusting habits; on occasions he would utilise the toilet facilities in the art school rather than brave using the bathroom in the flat.
For Kenny one additional attraction about the new arrangement was the chance to play Steven's extensive music collection. While Kenny had always loved music he seldom had enough cash to allow him to buy a new album and in any event living in Peterhead the selection was somewhat limited unless, of course, you were a big fan of Jim Reeves or the Alexander Brothers.

By the time that Kenny moved to Holburn Street it wasn't just his fellow students that were causing him concern. Before he went to the college he had several reservations centring on the likes of living away from home and securing a job to support himself. What had never given him a sleepless night was whether he would succeed; after all he had been the star art student at the Academy. Sadly all too quickly he realised that being the cream of Peterhead was somewhat different from excelling amongst people with real brilliance, the school's students being drawn from a rather larger talent pool. All too soon that villainous word to describe his abilities reared its ugly head again. Average.

He also began to have major concerns about what he would do if he managed to stagger through the course. If you graduated in one of the sciences or maths there countless fields of endeavour that would welcome you with open arms. Not so art. Okay you could go into advertising or teaching but the number of such jobs would clearly be limited and he suspected would quickly be filled with the top grade students of which he had to accept he was not one. Did he really want to spend several years of his life only to emerge into the real world to find himself stacking shelves fulltime, even if he was able to climb the ladder to performing such a task at the nearby more upmarket Sainsburys.

When he went home for that first Christmas he had already decided that unless he did brilliantly in the first year exams, which he greatly doubted, he would leave in summer. He tried to drop hints to his mother along those lines but she was so enamoured with the thought of having a son at Art School that she failed to pick up on them or if she did turned a deaf ear towards what was being suggested.

The results he achieved were even more mediocre than he had envisaged which in many ways made the decision to quit all the easier. The difficult thing was what to do with the rest of his life. He knew that his mother would be hugely disappointed and he vowed to try and find a job before he broke the news to her. He had spotted a notice in the staff room at Asda announcing that the store were looking for an assistant manager in the bakery department and although he concluded that he had little chance of success Kenny applied for it. Despite his tender years the powers that be were clearly impressed with his reliability and diligence and offered him the post on a three month trial basis.

When he broke the news to his mother about leaving the Arts School she took it far better than he had anticipated and he concluded that perhaps all along she had been picking up on the hints dropped around the Christmas table. Ever his greatest supporter she began to tell everyone who would listen that her darling boy was now a manager in a major store conveniently omitting the word 'assistant' and the fact that it was a trial.

The trial in fact lasted exactly three months at which time Kenny was officially appointed to the role. By that time his onetime stacking assistant, Steven, had also moved on, albeit in a very different direction. To the Holburn Bar, initially just serving behind the bar but eventually acting as their weekend D J, a task which Steven loved and which he would have been happy to do for free although he was quite willing to accept the fee on offer. Steven had been such a regular patron since the boys had set up home nearby that the manager had no reason to suspect that he was being a little economical with the truth when he provided a date of birth that suggested that he would be turning twenty in a couple of months time and not, as was the case, eighteen.

Despite the fact that both lads loved the independence that the flat provided neither felt totally comfortable amidst the student induced squalor and as soon as their greatly improved financial situation allowed they moved house, setting up home in a flat on Howburn Place, two minutes walk from the city's Union Street and yet providing easy access to Kenny's place of work. The flat was in a well maintained tenement and provided the desperately needed second bedroom. The building also had one other major attraction; it was student free.
Because Steven was needed in his dual roles of drinks dispenser and record spinner at weekends, the lads normally headed for the bright lights of the city during the week with a Thursday being a favourite night for them to party a little. And it was on one such day that life changed not only for Kenny but for both of them.

CHAPTER FOUR

Being a Thursday night the Fusion nightclub on Bridge Place wasn't exactly jam packed. It was in fact somewhat dead certainly at one a.m. by which time Steven was all for packing it in and heading for one of kebab take-a-ways on Windmill Brae that they would pass on their walk home. Kenny, however, was a little more reluctant.

Both had endeavoured to chat to some of the young and unattached girls with equal success. None. To Steven that wasn't much of an issue as he was regularly surrounded by members of the opposite sex anxious to catch the eye of the attractive DJ. For Kenny, however, it was a very different proposition. Despite that fact that he had been away from home for the better part of two years he remained a shy and introverted country lad who generally only seemed to have the confidence to speak to members of the opposite sex when his pal was there with him.

It was particularly galling for Kenny that evening as it had marked the unveiling of his new going-out outfit; a light grey suit with a three button jacket in the Italian style albeit bought from Burtons, a pale blue shirt and a dark blue tie which, he had to admit, had looked more alluring in the shop than under the disco lights. Being a shade thrifty he was reluctant to waste all that investment for no return and set about persuading his pal to give it just a little longer. Problem was that once Steven had been rebuffed a couple of times he took it as a personal insult and began to sulk.

Oh come on Kenny. Let's just admit this has been a waste of time. I could murder a kebab.
No, let's jist gie it anither ten minutes or so.
What's the point? We've had the brush off from practically every dame here. Well you certainly have anyway including a couple I didn't go near as I had forgotten my bargepole.
It's nae surprising you've hid nae success. As soon as they spot that tie you're wearin' they rin for the hills.
Rubbish!
No it's true. In fact I wish I hid brought my sunglasses.
What's wrong with my tie?
Dae you really wint me to tell you?
A tie like this makes a statement. Unlike that drab thing you've got on. This tie says something about me.
Aye it dis. It says 'I've got nae taste'.
And it attracts the girls.
Hisnae done a great job the night his it?

Secretly Kenny was resigned to the fact that Steven was right and it was time to cut their losses and head home. But the fact that the chance to go out with his great pal who provided him with Dutch courage wouldn't arise again for a week encouraged him to wait a little longer before throwing in the towel. And just at that moment a tall, blonde girl in an attractive mauve dress passed by him. He couldn't remember having seen her earlier and was pretty sure he would have noticed her. She took a seat at the bar and much to his surprise appeared to be quite alone.

He was convinced that she was unlikely to be interested in him but on the basis of nothing ventured he straightened his tie and was set to go and have a chat with her when Steven suddenly realised what was happening.

Where do you think you're going?
I'm goin' to say hello to the lassie that's sittin' over there.
The blonde? Bit out of your league is she not?
Oh thanks Steven.
That's what friends are for. To make sure you are realistic.
I'm nae worried fit you say. I'm gaen' to gie it a try.

Kenny was on his way over towards the girl when Steven suddenly grabbed his jacket.

Wait!
Oh come on now Steven. You ken the rules. I saw her first.
It's not that. I know her.
Rubbish.
I do. We were at the school together although she was a year ahead of me.
Okay so fit's her name then?
Oh I can't remember. Lorna or something like that. I went out with her.
You went oot wi' her?
Aye. On a few occassions. Total waste of time as it turned out.
She looks like a nice lassie.
That's the problem. I found out she was a nice lassie. I called her iron knickers at school after that and the name stuck.

Oh charming. Onywiy, I dinna care fit you say. I'm gaen to say hello.
Whatever. It's your funeral. And after she sees that tie you're wearing she'll probably think you've just come from one. And I've just remembered it's not Lorna. It's Lorraine. That's Lorraine Hunter.

CHAPTER FIVE

The arrival of a baby girl is generally a reason for rejoicing for most couples but seldom would it have been met with such unbridled euphoria as it was by Billy and Marilyn Hunter. Not that it was their first child; it was in fact the fifth little Hunter to arrive. It was, however, the first girl and after four boys Marilyn in particular had all but given up hope of having a daughter. She also knew that this would have to be their last addition to the family as their three bedroom semi on Summerhill Road was bursting at the seams and plans were already in hand to extend above the garage to provide another bedroom for this latest arrival.

With four older brothers Lorraine could have turned out as either as spoilt little princess or a tom boy and fortunately she opted for the later. By the time she was four she was already reluctant to wear the beautiful little dresses that her paternal grandmother, equally thrilled to have a girl in the family having given birth to two boys herself, would regularly buy for her. Indeed it was only with a considerable degree of coercion on her parents' part that Lorraine decreed to don them on a Sunday when they went visiting the grandparents. The rest of the time she would be decked out in a selection of hand-me-down Aberdeen or Scotland football jerseys which her Dad had bought for the boys.

And her interest in the beautiful game didn't stop there. Whenever there was a kick about in the back garden she would be there in the thick of it and even when her little bare legs were red from being constantly struck with the ball she would sniff back the tears and get on with it. By the time she was seven her brothers were wary of the little tornado that would charge around the garden, throwing herself into tackles, and occasionally leaving one of her older siblings prostrate on the grass.

Billy was in total awe of his daughter and thrilled that another Hunter was a football fan. His own love of the game dated back to his childhood and when league football in Scotland started to return to a degree of normality after the end of the Second World War his Dad began to take him to Pittodrie. Despite having been established for more than forty years Aberdeen F.C. had never won the Scottish Cup. Indeed bachelors in the city who were reluctant to get hitched would invariably respond to questions about their intentions by saying they would get married 'when Aberdeen win the cup'.
Having regularly accompanied his Dad to Pittodrie during that season he was beyond excitement when his father announced that he would be taking him to Hampden Park on the 19th of April 1947 for the Scottish Cup Final. He did, however, warn his twelve year son to be pragmatic about their team's chances and it was sound advice as their opponents, Hibernian, scored in the very first minute. Fortunately the Dons responded and two goals saw them lifting the cup for the first time in the history and an ecstatic Billy was there at the Joint Station to see the team return with their prize. Meantime a plethora of local young men were no doubt planning forthcoming nuptials.

Not surprisingly Billy became a devoted follower of his local team from that day forward and a regular season ticket holder. When his eldest boy, Archie, named after Archie Baird one of the stars of the cup winning outfit, turned twelve Billy decided to add a second season ticket and take him with him. Although excited by the prospect of going by half time in the inaugural outing to Pittodrie Archie was thoroughly bored and, having already consumed his bag of Pick n' Mix, asked if he could go home now. Convinced that the boy would grow to love it the pairing attended the next few home games until eventually Marilyn intervened on the boy's behalf to explain that he hated it and didn't want to go again.

Although disappointed Billy comforted himself with the thought that he had three other sons and asked Graham, named after star winger Graham Leggat, if he would like to accompany his father. Being less diplomatic than his older brother he simply answered no way, explaining that he was going with one of his teachers to watch Aberdeenshire playing cricket. Cricket, of all things; a sport that was regarded by Billy as being fundamentally English and therefore worthy of nothing but disdain.

Taking their cue from their elder brothers the two youngest male members of the Hunter clan quickly informed their father that they had no interest in sitting in the cold watching a bunch of men kicking a ball. A crestfallen Billy was contemplating who he could interest in buying the second season ticket when a little voice perked up with the words 'I'd like to go with you, Dad'.

While thrilled that someone would want to spend their Saturday afternoons with him Billy wasn't convinced that a football ground famed for its industrial language was the place for a seven year and a girl at that. But Lorraine, christened by her mother before Billy could come up with some strange adaption of an Aberdeen player's name, was so insistent that her Dad agreed that they could try it at the next home game, convinced that she would be fed up and never want to venture near the place again. Seven years later the two of them were a regular feature sitting side by side in the same two seats and it was only when Lorraine turned fourteen and began to get more interested in girly things, like boys, that the partnership was broken up.

But it wasn't just at the football that the Hunter clan enjoyed life together. Billy and Marilyn were stalwarts of Mannofield Church with Billy being an elder and his wife the reserve organist. There used to be an almost audible sigh of relief amongst the congregation when they saw Marilyn sitting on the organ stool as although self taught she was an accomplished musician. That made her somewhat different to Miss Jackson who had been the regular organist for many, many years and who still hadn't come close to mastering the instrument and with failing eyesight found it increasingly difficult to read the sheet music. When Miss Jackson was in the hot seat Billy would invariably trot out the famous Eric Morecambe quote about playing all the right notes but not necessarily in the right order.

The problem was that Miss Jackson had been there for so long, with one parishioner suggesting that she had once accompanied Methuselah, that no one had the heart to tell her that her services were no longer required.
With their Mum and Dad both expected to be at the Sunday morning service every week all other members of the family had no option but to attend. Most did it without complaint with Lorraine in particular enjoying the Sunday school as well as the Brownies and then the Guides; Lorraine was the type of girl who would happily join in with everything and do so with unbridled enthusiasm. But of course there is usually one black sheep in every family, especially when you have a flock of five, and in their case it was Tommy, the third son. He moaned about going to the kirk every single week and all the other members of the family were relieved when he turned fourteen and could be left 'home alone'.

It initially looked like Lorraine was going to adopt the physical attributes of her mother who was small and dumpy and as a consequence she barely generated a glance from the boys in Hazlehead Academy during her first two years. But then just like the dowdy waterfowl in Hans Christian Andersen's famous story she suddenly emerged as a beautiful swan. She stretched dramatically, losing her puppy fat in the process, and with her long straw coloured hair didn't so much as cause boys to give her a fleeting look but rather to stare in wonder.
By the time she was sixteen she was fighting them off but unlike many of her contemporaries she had no great wish to

'go steady'. Lots of the girls in her school year were baffled by the number of invites she turned down and even more so when, after a couple of dates, she suddenly dumped the 'dishy' Steven Grant.

By the time Lorraine was seventeen two of her brothers had already left home to attend Universities in Strathclyde and Stirling and her parents thought that she might be inclined to follow the same path. Lorraine was confident that she could achieve grades that would get her into a University but not one of a sufficiently high standard to allow her to study the likes of law or medicine. She had known too many people who had gone to Uni emerging after three years with degrees in Drama or Film Studies or Sociology only to find that the only job waiting for them was waitressing in some cafe and she had no wish to end up like them.

She had a keen interest in politics inherited from her Dad who regularly stood, unsuccessfully it has to be said, for the S.N.P. in the Hazlehead ward at the local council elections and she had spent many an evening tramping round the streets popping leaflets through letterboxes. As she was approaching the end of her fifth year she alerted her careers master to the fact that she had shelved any idea of going onto to further education and would be looking for a job. He was well aware of her interest in politics as whenever any debate took place in the classroom Lorraine always came alive fervently spelling out the case for an independent Scotland. He brought to her attention a post being advertised by the local Council for an assistant to Councillors which she applied for and, much to her surprise was appointed to the role. Her Dad was thrilled

until he learned that the two Councillors she would be working for were both Tories.
She was initially concerned that her parents would be disappointed in her decision not to head for a University. In fact nothing could have been further from the truth as they were both thrilled that the baby of the family wasn't following in her brothers' footsteps and leaving home. And when she did depart from the family abode more than three years later it was not to the central belt but only to central Aberdeen.

Lorraine enjoyed working in the Town House and when she had a spare minute would wander round the beautiful historic building, looking at the portraits of the many men who had held the prestigious post of Lord Provost although a little disappointed that there wasn't a single women amongst them. She also loved the hustle and bustle of local politics and the only aspect of her political life that she didn't relish were the civic receptions where she would have to mingle and engage in small talk with invited guests many of whom over indulged in the free alcohol on offer.
It was at one such night that she first made the acquaintance of a girl who was circulating amongst the assembled gathering proffering a tray of canapés. Lorraine had found herself trapped by a middle aged man with bad breath and even worse dress sense who got closer and closer to her with each passing minute. It was when he briefly turned to speak to someone else that she made her escape doing so with such alacrity that she bumped in to the tray-bearing waitress.

I'm so sorry.
That's okay Madam.
It's just that...
You saw a chance to flee. And I wouldn't blame you.
He's old enough to be my father.
I must admit that the age thing doesn't bother me. I just don't find beer bellies and hair plastered down with a jar of Brylcreem attractive.
And you forgot the halitosis added Lorraine which caused both girls to burst out laughing *I'm Lorraine.*
Paula
Well that's not an Aberdeen accent anyway.
No I'm from Glasgow. I'm up here studying at RGU and doing these odd waitressing jobs to try and keep my head above water.
And are you enjoying life in Aberdeen?
Well yes and no. I love the Uni course but I didn't get into the halls of residence and I am not happy living in a hostel. I am desperate to move into a flat but need to find someone to share the cost with. You don't know anyone do you? Sorry if that is inappropriate.
Not at all. Actually I might just know someone. Can we meet for a coffee sometime and chat about it?

And she did know someone. A girl by the name of Lorraine Hunter who realised that having turned twenty-one the time had come for her to fly the nest. When she and Paula met for a coffee two days later the idea of getting a place together just snowballed and within weeks a suitable flat was located on St

Andrews Street. In a whirlwind Lorraine found herself packing her possessions including her beloved 'lucky' red and white bar scarf and heading to the first home of her own.
The girls got on well together despite the fact that they were very different. Paula was a party girl and would have been out every night of the week if she wasn't permanently hard up. Lorraine on the other hand was quite content to curl up in the flat with a good book and her flatmate liked to rib her by suggesting that she should get herself a cat so that she would be ready for spinsterhood.
But that certainly wasn't a scenario that Lorraine was planning for. Having been raised in the bosom of a loving family she wanted little more from life than a husband, when Mr. Right eventually appeared, and a couple of kids perhaps topped off with a dog, not being a fan of felines. Despite enjoying the quiet life from time to time Paula did manage to persuade her to put down her latest book and go out for an evening.

CHAPTER SIX

Lorraine had noticed the guy eyeing her up as she returned from the toilet. He certainly was not a heart throb but looked pleasant with a kind face and she wouldn't have been averse to chatting to him if he made his move. However, when she glanced over a few minutes later he appeared to have lost interest and was deep in conversation with his mate who most certainly could have been described as eye candy. Despite the dim lights in the night club there was something familiar looking about that guy but she couldn't remember if she knew him or if he just reminded her of someone.
She was still trying to place the mystery guy when a few moments later she felt a tap on her shoulder which roused her from her revere and alerted her to the fact that she had company.

Hi. I wondered if I could buy you a drink?
How do you know that my boyfriend isn't off getting me one?
Sorry. I didn't mean to bother you if you are here with someone.
It's okay. I'm just winding you up. I am here with someone but it's a girlfriend who is off chatting to some guy. So yes I could murder a G & T.

While Kenny was off fetching the drinks Lorraine took the time to study the other guy. It was then it dawned on her just who it was; it was someone she had been at school with and who brought back brief but unpleasant memories.

Here's your drink. By the way I'm Kenny.
And I'm ....
Lorraine. Aye I ken.
I take it HE told you.
Aye my pal Steven telt me.
Steven Grant. So you're friends with him?
Aye.
Really sorry to hear that.
Steven's fine.
That's not how I would describe him.
He said you wint out wi' him a few times.
Twice! And no doubt he told you that he dumped me?
Well...
Thought so. It was in fact the other way round. And did he also happen to reveal the charming nickname that he invented for me and spread round the school.
He sort of mentioned it.
But conveniently forgot about my revenge no doubt. The Octopus.
Is that fit you caed him?
Yup.
But why?
You obviously never sat in the back row of the pictures with him or you wouldn't need to ask.

Kenny, who was often shy around girls, suddenly felt relaxed with this lassie although the several drinks he had consumed undoubtedly helped. They spoke about this and that until Lorraine drained her glass.

Anyway thanks for the drink but I think I should be getting up the road.
Wid you like company?
Yes that would be nice.
But fit aboot your frien'?
Who Paula? That's her over there with the red and green top.
Wi' the guy wi' the baldie heid?
Aye that's her.
He's a bittie auld for her is he nae.
No she likes them mature. She says that she only draws the line if they insist in taking their Zimmer frame with them. She loves coming her on a Thursday as she reckons it a 'grab a granddad 'night.
So dae you wint to tell her your awa'?
No the way she is hanging around Kojak I don't think she'll be lonely tonight.
Richt I'll jist let Steven ken fit's happening.

As Kenny approached his pal Lorraine tried to hang back in the hope that Steven wouldn't spot her but she was out of luck.

Look who it is. Little Lorraine. Still trying to find a man?
Yes Steven. Still trying to act like one?

So you two remember each ither? interjected a clearly embarrassed Kenny.

Oh aye. Steven is hard to forget. But well worth the effort.

And I take it you are still living with Mummy and Daddy Lorraine?

Actually no. I am sharing a flat on St Andrews Street with a friend.

Kenny, a word of warning if you are seeing her home don't go up George Street or you'll never get Lorraine past Finnie the Jewellers if they've got a window display of engagement rings.

CHAPTER SEVEN

Castlemilk is not a name that is likely to crop up in any Visit Scotland literature. The housing scheme in the south side of Glasgow was initially designed to accommodate people being re-housed when the notorious Gorbals scheme was demolished. It quickly became a place to live in not to visit and Paula Webster lived within its boundaries from the day she was born until a month before her twentieth birthday.

Paula's Dad was in many ways a model parent compared with many of her contemporaries' fathers. He was reliable and enjoyed steady and reasonably well paid work as a driver with Bluebird buses and he didn't smoke or drink to excess. He had just the one failing and one that was derived from an incident in his teenage years. When he was eighteen he accompanied his friend Gordon into a bookmaker, his first visit to such an establishment, and just for the fun of it he decided to risk a whole ten shillings on a horse race.
Having studied the list of horses due to run in the 2:30 at Chepstow he decided to put his money on a horse called *Rothesay Lad*, choosing that particular nag simply because his grandmother loved to talk about spending her summer holidays on that resort in Bute. When Gordon, who studied the Sporting Post religiously every day, saw his pal's selection he burst out laughing pointing out that it was rank outsider with odds of 25 to 1 and that he would be as well putting his money down the drain outside. Fifteen minutes later it was

Robert Webster that was laughing as he suddenly found that he had more money in his pocket than he had ever seen in his short life.

From that day forth he endeavoured to repeat that feat but sadly with very limited success. There was the occasional good day but those were heavily outweighed by the bad ones. He would listen intently to people who would point out that the local bookie was driving around in a flashy new Jag while Robert cycled to work on a daily basis. And then the next day he would go out and put a wad of hard earned cash on some filly that 'couldn't possibly fail to win' but yet found some way to do just that. As a consequence some Christmases were wonderful with Lorraine receiving gifts that most kids were jealous of while in other years Santa apparently couldn't find his way to the Webster home.

Paula's mother was a very different person. For as long as Paula could remember her Mother had suffered from bouts of depression which were hardly helped by the fact that her husband's gambling habit created a permanent air of doubt about whether bills could be paid. Agnes Webster hated having to go out to work, not because she was inherently lazy, although house work had never appealed to her, but simply because she found it very difficult to mix with people when she was feeling down. Unfortunately the uncertainty of her husband bringing home sufficient money to keep them solvent and keep the bailiffs from their door meant that she had no option but to find part time employment in some of the local shops.

Lorraine had two much older siblings, Sheila and Ernie. Sheila worked on the cosmetics counter at Lewis's Departmental Store on Argyle Street and as result was always beautifully made up which was somewhat different to Paula who got herself ready in the morning by simply giving her hair a quick brush. Ernie on the other hand had an aversion to hard work or work of any kind, preferring to help himself to other people's goods. After twice getting off with a warning and a fine he was eventually sentenced to a period of incarceration or 'three months at her Majesty's pleasure' as his Dad like to describe it. Lorraine was only ten at the time that happened and was confused as to what pleasure the Queen, who she thought looked like a kind old lady, could possibly derive from locking up a young lad.

With a sister and a brother ten and eight years older than her respectively, Paula was the baby of the family and as a consequence totally spoiled especially by her doting dad. But then out the blue, or so it seemed to her, a baby arrived on the scene and she was horrified when she discovered that it wasn't just visiting but was in fact there to stay. Alfred, as he was named, was tiny weighing in at a mere five pounds six ounces leaving her Dad to joke that he had been stuck with the runt of the litter. When she was older Paula was given full chapter and verse about her behaviour in the early weeks of Alfie's life during which time neither her mother nor father chanced leaving her and the baby in the same room in case Paula did something evil to it.

As he grew, slowly, Paula and Alfie became almost inseparable as a consequence of their closeness in age and

Paula got herself into countless scrapes and fights both at primary and secondary schools defending her wee brother who was always the smallest in his classes. His diminutive stature lead to a great deal of speculation amongst the neighbours as to whether Robert Webster was really his biological father but anyone who looked closely at them when they were out together would have had no doubts to that effect as facially they were like two peas in a pod.

In most places the Webster family would probably have been described as dysfunctional; in Castlemilk they could be referred to as normal.

Paula was eleven years old and in the last few weeks of attending the local primary school before she ventured beyond the boundaries of the city of Glasgow, going on a one day bus trip with her class. They went to Ayr and it was the first time she had seen the sea or sand and she was simply ecstatic about the experience. Indeed it eventually changed her life.
Back in school the following week the teacher began asking all the children what they wanted to do when they grew up. Most of the boys went along the predictable route of ‘play for Rangers’ or ‘be a fireman’, the girls ‘become an air hostess’ or ‘a hairdresser’. When it came to Paula’s turn she simply replied ‘to leave Castlemilk’ and she was bemused by the laughter her answer generated. Her classmates clearly thought she was trying to be funny when in fact she was deadly serious.

Paula stayed on at school until she was seventeen as opposed to most of the other local girls of her age who would leave aged fifteen or sixteen, often pushing a pram. She had hoped that by completing a fifth year she would secure examination passes that would propel her into a University and thereby release her from the confines of Castlemilk. Sadly it was not to be although she came close, near enough to allow her to explore another route that of attending Glasgow Clyde College to study for an HNC degree in Biology, one of her favoured subjects at school. She choose the option of studying part time for two years, as opposed to the one year full time course, as it allowed her get a part time work that would help her to build her nest egg before she moved away.

Contentedly ensconced at the College she went in search of a suitable job and quickly found one, working as a waitress in an upmarket Italian restaurant in Glasgow's trendy Merchant City quarter. The establishment was owned by a second generation Italian named Luigi who addressed customers in a broken accent making it sound like he had just arrived from Napoli that day; the rest of the time he spoke in a broad Glasgow tongue that sounded much more like Billy Connolly than Silvio Berlusconi.

Paula found that he was a decent boss and one that paid well providing you were willing to graft which she most certainly was and she soon became a favourite amongst restaurant regulars who enjoyed her attentive service. Luigi was also delighted with his young protégée who returned a higher 'per

plate' rate than any of the other serving staff. It was only after watching her for a few nights that he discovered her secret.
As the night wore on and large groups of customers became a little 'merry' Paula would be there to not only constantly fill up their wine glasses but to offer to fetch another bottle of the vino and in their inebriated state they were generally happy to go along with the suggestion. The wee lassie from the tenements of Castlemilk also had one more little trick up her sleeve; as she was pouring the wine she would proffer the bottle with a serving cloth round the bottom pretending that it was empty despite the fact that there was usually close to a glass of wine remaining. That endeared her to her fellow workers who would 'dispose' of the residue in these bottles at the end of the night when the last of the customers had gone. Luigi was also happy to turn a blind eye to this sharp practice because of the extra money it brought in.
But he also had another reason for not carpeting Paula and it had nothing to do with her abilities as a waitress. Despite the fact that he was only in his mid thirties Luigi was already divorced and clearly looking for female companionship. At school Paula had been decidedly disinterested in the boys who generally seemed to be burdened with an overdeveloped libido and a spectacular display of acne and after she left she continued to be more attracted to males of the mature variety. Despite a waistline that displayed his fondness for pasta she found Luigi quite attractive and was happy to go out with him on a Monday night when the restaurant was closed.
Over the course of the next few months she enjoyed evenings at the theatre and the cinema and even the opera which, much

to her surprise, she really loved. The nights out concluded with a pleasant supper and always without her ever opening her handbag except to re-apply a coat of lipstick. But all good things must come to an end and when he began to talk of moving in together she decided that the time had come to move on.

She found a job in another city centre restaurant where the pay was even better and the owner was a fat old man devoted to his wife, children and grand kids and she remained there until she had successfully completed the HNC course.

Having achieved that objective Paula then had to decide on which Universities she would apply to for a place, a situation greatly complicated by her obsession, arising from a single day trip to Ayr many years before, with moving somewhere by the sea that had a beach. That substantially narrowed down the options to basically St Andrews and the two Unis in Aberdeen. It was no great surprise when the ancient establishment in Fife very quickly rejected her approach but she was more than a little disappointed when Aberdeen University followed suit.

Fortunately Robert Gordon's University or RGU offered her a place to study Biomedical Science which she instantly accepted. She was beyond excited to break the news to her parents but unfortunately their reaction didn't match her expectations. Although her Dad said that he was happy for her it was clear that he still viewed her as his little girl and was worried about her going so far away from her family home. Her mother on the other hand made no effort to disguise the fact that she was very far from impressed although in her case it had nothing to do with losing her daughter. While Paula had been studying in Glasgow she had been contributing to the household income from her waitressing which had allowed her mother to avoid working and to hide away in the house. The thought that the contributions from Paula would cease and that she would have to get off the sofa and back into the labour market didn't please her mother at all.

There was, however, one person who was genuinely thrilled with Paula's success and that was her paternal grandmother. In the girl's eyes she was the archetypical perfect Gran, sweet and kind, and from an early age Paula had never needed to be coerced into visiting her. Gran Webster was overjoyed when she heard about the girl's success especially as Paula was the first person in her family and, even better than that, all her close friends' families to be accepted into a 'real University' as she loved to refer to it. She had difficulty in getting her mind and tongue around the Biomedical Science description of the course and simply told everyone willing to listen, and a few who weren't, that her granddaughter was going all the way to Aberdeen to study an 'ology', mimicking the Maureen Lipman TV advert popular at the time.

On the day that Paula was due to leave her Gran turned up with a small parcel for her containing a woollen scarf she had knitted (*because it's awfley cauld up there*), a packet of tea bags, clearly convinced that there wouldn't be proper shops in Aberdeen, two Mars bars and a five pound note. The gesture reduced Paula to tears and from then on she ensured that on her Grandmother's birthday Interflora always turned up at her house.

Thanks to having saved every penny she could during her two years at College Paula had a reasonably impressive bank balance when she arrived in the North East but was dismayed when she realised that accommodation in a city in the grip of an oil boom was far more expensive than she had anticipated. How things would have turned out if she hadn't quickly secured a waitressing job and met Lorraine Hunter she didn't know. She was just eternally grateful that fate had dealt her a decent hand and that she not only had somewhere safe to stay but that she had acquired a new best friend in the process.

CHAPTER EIGHT

It was when Kenny announced that he was leaving half way through a particularly lively domino session that Steven knew for certain that his pal was a goner. It was almost as if Kenny was walking around the pub brandishing a 'The End is Nigh' sandwich board. It was that obvious.

Being tall and well built Steven became a regular in a centre back role in the Hazlehead Academy school football team, picked week in, week out by the sports master and team coach, 'Baldy' Thomson despite Steven's behaviour. Despite turning up later than all his team mates for most games. Despite skipping training sessions when he simply couldn't be bothered. The story went about the school that 'Baldy' was able to boast a full head of luxurious hair until Steven Grant came along.
He had more final warnings than any boy deserved, a fact that Steven would readily admit to, even surviving when the team kicked off with only ten men on one occasion as Steven was round the back of the changing rooms having a fag. But everyone knew that the day would come when the coach would blow his hirsute deprived top and so it proved. He gave Steven a dressing down in front of all his team mates suggesting that unless he 'pulled up his socks' he was off the team. The bold hero, quite unchastened, responded by suggesting that perhaps Mr. Thomson needed to visit an optician as, if he cared to look, he would notice that Steven's

socks were in fact pulled up as far as they could possibly go. When the team sheet for the next game was pinned up on the school notice board the name of S. Grant was, not surprisingly, absent.

Steven was quite unconcerned by this turn of events as he was becoming bored with playing anyway. He had made friends with a few older pupils in their sixth year at the school who invited him to join them on their weekly pastime of going to watch the local football team and so a regular Saturday custom began. They would meet in the Stewart Lounge on Correction Wynd at two o'clock every Saturday and have a pint before heading for Pittodrie to watch the first team if they were at home and the reserves if they weren't. After the game they would all troop back to the pub for a couple more pints of McEwen's Export and a serious session of dominoes. That was the routine, come rain or shine, every Saturday with the exception of the dreaded close season.

Not long after they had moved into their first flat together Steven persuaded Kenny, who he knew was a keen football fan, to join them on a Saturday if he wasn't working. Kenny loved it and not just the actual games but the whole day out. He was quickly welcomed into the group and enjoyed the warm and friendly atmosphere in the Stewart Lounge. He even became quite adept at the strange art of domino playing although he remained silently amused about how seriously some of his fellow players took the game which to him was ninety percent luck, ten percent skill.

He therefore hated to leave early on that Saturday just prior to Christmas but he had made a promise and he wasn't going to let Lorraine down by failing to turn up or even by turning up having drunk too much, although the later had its attractions; it would numb the pain of what lay ahead.

Lads, I'm awa'
Kenny, you don't actually have to tell us every time you go to the loo.
I'm nae aff to the toilet. I'm awa' hame to get changed. I'm meetin' Lorraine in an hour's time.
But it's only half past five.
I ken. I can read a watch. But we're gaen to the early show at the theatre.
The theatre? What's on anyway?
Cinderella.
A pantomime! You must be joking.
No, I'm nae. Lorraine's Grunny boucht her tickets.
Well good luck son. You'll certainly need it.

Steven meant every word as he hated the theatre with a passion. It all emanated from the time when he was ten and his mother and father, unable to find anyone willing to stay with their darling boy, dragged him along to His Majesty's. Scottish Opera, of whom Mummy and Daddy were naturally jolly keen patrons, were in town and Steven was forced to spend hours listening to a group of people bawling their lungs out in a foreign language which he, and to his mind most of the other audience members, didn't understand. Contrary to what he had been led to believe it wasn't all over when the fat

lady sang as she insisted on repeating that task over and over again.
On his way home that night he answered his father's query about whether he had enjoyed it by informing him that he would rather have spent the evening at the dentist having root canal treatment. He vowed there and then never to go near a theatre again and had faithfully adhered to that promise. But in truth he would rather have sat through another opera than a pantomime. Although he had never obviously seen one live he had caught glimpses of them on T.V. and couldn't believe that people would actually pay good money to watch a bunch of second rate actors, who seemed to disappear from the public's gaze for the rest of the year, engaging in cross dressing for some inexplicable reason and churning out terrible parodies of popular songs and an endless stream of dire jokes that wouldn't even grace a Christmas cracker.
Kenny wasn't looking forward to the Pantomime very much either but he was going to please Lorraine who in turn was only there because of her Granny who had once taken Lorraine to see a Panto. Lorraine had loved it so much her Granny decided to give her a treat by buying her tickets. Problem is that Lorraine was six at the time she first went and her tastes had changed more than a little since then.

Although it was less than a fifteen minute walk from the Fusion nightclub to Lorraine's flat in St Andrews Street Kenny was already smitten by the attractive and vivacious young lady he was escorting home for the first time that night and was delighted when she agreed to accompany him to the cinema the next day. Lorraine wasn't quite so instantly enamoured by the lad with the 'teuchter' accent but he seemed pleasant and well mannered and, unlike so many of the men who had walked her home, wasn't suddenly all over her like a rash, settling for a gentle peck on the cheek.

Lorraine left the choice of cinema viewing to Kenny. Having glanced at the Evening Express 'what's on' column she was sure that he would opt for 'A View to Kill', the latest James Bond movie. She wasn't a fan of car chases and gun fights and was therefore more than a little surprised, although delighted, when he suggested that they go for another 'view' altogether, 'A Room With A View', a bittersweet romance set in Venice. It was at that stage that she realised that this new boyfriend, if that was what he was going to become, was a real romantic and that suited Lorraine just fine.

It quickly developed from going out together to the cinema, Kenny's favourite, or for a quick drink which Lorraine preferred, to meeting up whenever possible. Problem was that although Kenny had been elevated from assistant to Bakery Manager at Asda, much to his mother's delight who quickly commenced another round of spreading the good news, he still had to adhere to shift work and often didn't finish until it was too late in the evening for the couple to meet up. On the other hand when he had days off during the week he became a regular sight outside the Town House at a lunchtime waiting for Lorraine so they could nip down to one of the many nearby eateries for a quick bite to eat and a catch up. Indeed he became such a habitual visitor at the Council building that he was quickly on first name terms with most of the staff.

It was when he was first invited by Lorraine to come and meet her parents that he realised that he had his feet firmly under the table. He found them to be charming and got on particularly well with her Dad, a long time season ticket holder at Pittodrie. Billy quizzed the young lad about his football loyalties and was mighty relieved when he was able to ascertain that Kenny also went to Pittodrie and wasn't one of those folk from the Blue Toon who professed to supporting one of the two big clubs from Glasgow, particularly the one whose name should not be spoken in the Hunter household.

A month later, on a Sunday when Kenny was not working, the couple journeyed to Peterhead to meet the Mutches and Jean was thrilled by her son's choice of girlfriend especially when she learned that the couple had deliberately caught the early morning bus so that they could accompany her to church. After the service Jean hung back so that she could not only shake hands with the Minister but introduce him to her son's 'intended'.

Back at the house she unveiled a spread which Kenny reckoned would have fed half of Peterhead as well as a few folk from Boddam and St. Fergus but was apparently intended only for the five members of the immediate family that had gathered. Jean had been keen on inviting her sister and family and, of course, cousin Rhona but fortunately had revealed her plan to Kenny prior to the day and he had been able to persuade her to keep it simple so that Lorraine wouldn't be overwhelmed. Although Jean was more than a little disappointed at not being able to show off the girl she reluctantly agreed.

So the romance blossomed to the extent that Kenny was willing to even suffer an evening of listening to strange people shouting out 'behind you Buttons' although he did need a stiff drink, or three, after that particular experience. Following a quiet Hogmanay, a part of the year that Lorraine hated, the couple looked forward to a new year and the possibility of enjoying a first holiday together. Money was tight so any thoughts of visiting the Big Apple or Disney World were placed in a 'to do' drawer to be revisited when finances allowed. Although they spent many a spring evening browsing through a selection of holiday magazines Kenny did that somewhat half heartedly as he already had his own plan in place.

As soon as April Come She Will, as songwriter Paul Simon succinctly put it, and daffodils were providing a feast of spring colour, Kenny got to work, realising that it was less than three months until the big date, 24 June, the anniversary of when Lorraine and him had first met. First step was to contact the various people whose help and assistance he would have to engage and he began with Anne, Lorraine's boss at the City Council. Having divulged his intentions she happily altered the holiday rota.
Next up was Marilyn. The previous September Lorraine had gone off on a family holiday to Italy, an occurrence which didn't thrill Kenny but had been booked long before they had met. As a result he knew that Lorraine had a passport, a document which he had acquired for himself, but needed to ensure that Lorraine's one still boasted a valid date. Marilyn

also discreetly prepared a bag of her daughter's summer tops and dresses and swimwear, keeping it hidden in a wardrobe in her bedroom until it was required.

The third person Kenny approached to be part of the subterfuge was Paula. Although initially a little wary of the flatmate Kenny had warmed to her, growing accustomed to her caustic wit, and he involved her in what was probably the most important part of the ploy. Creating a spurious excuse for not being able to meet Lorraine for lunch on one of his days off Kenny met up with Paula at the premises of Finnie the Jewellers, an establishment that Lorraine and him often window shopped at as they passed by.

It was clear that the jewellers had a vast selection of engagement rings but that a sizeable number of them were out with his limited budget. Without the erudite advice of Paula he would probably have left the shop with something very showy and colourful but totally unsuitable. His confidant, however, pointed him the direction of a ring which was simple and classy in the form of a solitaire diamond and one which he could afford. Just. With the agreement of the shop that it could be exchanged if the lady who he hoped would become his fiancée didn't like it he departed much poorer but much happier.

That left only one piece of the jigsaw to fit in; where to go on holiday. Again he sought professional advice by dropping in to a Thomas Cook travel agency where it was explained to him that if he wanted a week in the sun flying from Aberdeen that the selection was somewhat limited. Very limited in fact.

They could fly to Malaga and head for Torremolinos or to Alicante and holiday in Benidorm. Having never been south of Glasgow, and that was only for a game at Hampden, hc found the choice difficult and opted for the later because it was a slightly shorter flight and, more importantly, it was cheaper.

With everything in place Kenny was ready to take Lorraine to Spain, getting there, on a plane.

CHAPTER NINE

Football manager Tommy Docherty once famously quipped that he had had more clubs than Jack Nicklaus. Steven Grant could have claimed something similar although in his case it would be night clubs not football clubs he was referring to. Having made a name for himself as a DJ in the Holburn Bar it was not surprising that he was head hunted by another local hostelry and from there to another in the bustling Belmont Street area. Steven transferred his allegiance not because he had any disagreement with his current employers but for one reason only. Money.

Steven was a spendthrift who particularly loved designer clothes. To Kenny clothes were something that kept him warm and reasonably respectable although things did improve when Lorraine came on the scene. For a start she managed to get him to condemn the corduroy green jacket he had bought in a sale and which, in addition to being a bilious colour, had the disadvantage of being three sizes too big for him.

Steven wouldn't have been seen dead in the type of establishment that Kenny frequented and instead was a very regular visitor to Kakfa and other city centre boutiques who took great delight in selling clothes at hugely inflated prices. Not that Steven worried about the cost. As long as it had a crocodile or a horse logo on the chest or a detachable label on one sleeve he was happy, content in the knowledge that everyone who saw him would know that his clothes cost a lot.

But it wasn't just fashion that caused Steven to dig deep in his pockets. Whenever anything new came along he always had to have it first and was standing in the queue at Bruce Miller's the day that the first video cassette recorder came on the scene and seldom a day would go by without him adding to his rapidly expanding library of video cassettes. Kenny tried to persuade him that most of the titles could be hired for a fraction of the cost of buying the cassette which made much more sense bearing in mind that he probably wouldn't watch them more than once but Steven, who loved possessions, wouldn't be convinced.

On his return from his lunchtime visit to the jewellers Kenny found Steven in his usual spot, draped across the settee watching a movie. He looked slightly surprised when he saw Kenny enter apparently empty handed.

I thought you were going shopping?
I did go.
Oh. Was British Home Stores shut?
Ignoring the jibe Kenny fetched the precious little ring box from his pocket and displayed its contents to his flat mate.
Very nice. But I don't think it would suit you Kenny.
Dae you think she will say yes?
Who?
Lorraine, of course.
I don't think you need to worry. Lorraine has been looking for an engagement ring since she was at school. Primary school. So when do you intend popping the question?

When we're on holiday.
Of course you're off to sunny Spain aren't you? Is it Torremolinos you're going to?
No I've telt you a dizen times. It's Benidorm.
Same difference. So when do you leave?
Friday morning.
That's not going to give you long to practice.
Practice fit?
The 'Agadoo' song, of course. Did the travel agent not warn you that you won't get into Benidorm unless you know every word and gesture?

Kenny had never been in an airport let alone a plane and was fascinated by the Departures and Arrivals boards in Aberdeen Airport even if most of the destinations listed were no more glamorous than Wick and Stavanger. But there in the middle shining like a beacon was the name of Alicante and the renewed nerves he felt necessitated yet another visit to the toilet. When he returned to his seat in the waiting area Lorraine was still sitting there flicking through a copy of Vogue magazine and looking totally relaxed like a consummate seasoned traveller.
Then suddenly they were being called to board the plane and before long Kenny was starring out of the window in wonder as they passed by famous landmarks like the Blackpool Tower. Three hours later as they descended the steps they were met by a blast of hot air. Having been brought up in a place where the maxim 'never cast a clout 'til May be out'

was strictly adhered to his first encounter with a temperature of ninety degrees literally took his breath away.
While most of his fellow passengers were desperate to get to their hotel and get stuck into the bevy Kenny was simply entranced by everything he saw from the bus taking them to their destination and was in truth quite happy to be one of the last to reach their hotel as it gave him a chance to see Benidorm. It may not have been one of Europe's beauty spots but to someone used to a day out in Cruden Bay it was special.
He was equally thrilled by their hotel and loved their room on the tenth floor especially the large balcony with the promised view of the Mediterranean; okay it was somewhat distant view but for a loon who loved to be beside the sea it was perfect. They quickly unpacked and headed for the pool where Lorraine immediately began working on her tan. Kenny on the other hand, always a bit scared for himself, covered every inch of his pale skin in case he would get burned.
Their first evening was spent at a pavement cafe close by their hotel. Lorraine was thrilled by the balmy air, the ambience of the place and the chance to 'people watch'. Kenny was thrilled by the prices. He had been told that Spain was cheap but a pint of lager for what, after a great deal of calculation involving pesetas and pounds, was little more than fifty pence was even better than he had hoped for.
They quickly adopted a routine. Days were spent at the pool followed by a brief visit to beach with a paddle in the warm Med waters and then back to the pool although some days Lorraine gave the beach a miss as she hated the fact that sand

got everywhere. Evenings comprised of a browse around the various market stalls that sprung up as the sun went down followed by a meal at restaurant. Kenny knew he would never tire of being able to eat outside until late wearing just a T shirt and shorts.

All too soon Kenny realised that they had reached the special date of June 24th when he had to put his planned strategy into action. Before he had left home he had practiced what to say many times even going down on one knee in front of a mirror to ensure that he didn't look like a pillock. Settled at their favourite restaurant he broke out and ordered the second cheapest bottle of house wine and steaks for them both unaware that Lorraine had avoided doing just that wary of the possibility that they might end up eating something that had once run in the 4.30 at Kempston.

The time for the big moment arrived and it was only then that Kenny realised that the tables were so close together that even if he could go down on one knee that he would probably have great difficulty getting back to his seat with any degree of elegance and without knocking over the adjacent table. In any event he really didn't want to be the centre of attention in such a busy restaurant.

And so the planned speech was jettisoned and from a seated position he simply blurted out *maybe we should get engaged sometime* to which Lorraine replied *aye maybe we should.* As far as romantic exchanges were concerned it was hardly an extract from *Romeo & Juliet* but it did the purpose and he immediately handed over the ring box. Lorraine took one look at the contents and burst into tears causing Kenny to blurt out *if you dinna like it, it can easy be exchanged.* By that time Lorraine had it on her finger where it fitted perfectly thanks to the foresight of Paula and eventually though the tears she told him that it was *just perfect.*

The couple at the adjoining table quickly worked out what was going on and alerted the waiter who subsequently returned with a bottle of Champagne, or some Spanish equivalent, which was *on the 'ouse.* Kenny was delighted although it made him wonder if he should have proposed before he had ordered their bottle of wine.

Lorraine had difficulty in finishing her meal as she stopped every couple of minutes to stare at her ring, viewing it from every conceivable angle and in every possible light. Two days later they were on the plane heading back to Scotland which was in grip of an unseasonably cold and wet spell but Lorraine didn't care a fig as all she wanted to do was get home so she could show off her ring to everybody she knew.

CHAPTER TEN

Lorraine's parents were thrilled when they learned of the engagement as they had always made it clear that they wouldn't be too happy if the couple set up house together before they were married. As Lorraine had no wish to upset them in any way she had quickly squashed Kenny's veiled suggestion of co-habiting and for that reason they decided that they wouldn't delay getting hitched. They soon discovered, however, that they were far from being the only people keen on a spring wedding and they just couldn't find a suitable venue.

November, however, was an entirely different proposition as few couples seemed interested in their big day being held in that cold, dark and bleak month. But needs must and after traipsing around several possible locations for the reception they opted for the Amatola Hotel in Aberdeen.

Over the three years of her RGU course and the months since Paula had secured a job she loved in the forensic laboratory at Grampian Police HQ on Queen Street, Lorraine and her had become best pals. While Kenny wouldn't have been her personal choice as a boyfriend Paula liked the guy and knew that he would be good for her pal. She was therefore overjoyed when a wedding date was set and she was even more thrilled to be asked to be bridesmaid.

Steven was remarkably emotional about being invited to be best man; as an only child Kenny was as close to a brother as

he had ever had and he was genuinely taken aback and humbled by the request. What Kenny didn't tell him was that he had had to fight tooth and nail, even putting up with a day of Lorraine's sulking, before his future wife accepted the position. While Lorraine no longer harboured the degree of animosity towards Steven that she had felt when they were at school she would never be a fan of the guy. But if that was her fiancé's choice then so be it.
Steven and Paula had only met once before when the four of them had gone out for meal together and it had proved a rather frosty and not terribly enjoyable experience and one, for that very reason, that was never repeated. In light of the fact that they were to be the chief attendants to the main couple, or as Steven in his cynical way liked to describe it the *chief mourners,* he felt that Paula and him should get to know each other better before performing their duties. And so a week before the big day the couple met and shared a bottle of merlot in one of the fancy wine bars that had sprung up in the centre of town. Perhaps fuelled by the alcohol they found that they rather enjoyed each other's company.

So I assume that your pal Lorraine has told you all about me?
Well...
Can I just say that only 95% of it is true? Kenny on the other hand has said remarkably little about you. So come on, tell me about yourself? With that accent you are clearly not a local.
No I'm from Glasgow.
I thought you sounded like a weegie. Someone once told me that there are only two things that Glasgow is famous for.

And what are they?
Attractive women and good football players.
They could be right.
So tell me, what position do you play?
Paula couldn't help herself and burst out laughing, further warming the atmosphere.
You cheeky brute!
So how did you end up in Aberdeen?
I got a place at RGU.
You must have passed quite a few universities and colleges on the way up. Why here?
Because of the beach and the sea.
You're joking!
No. Do you not like going to the beach?
Aye. The ones in the Med. Not Aberdeen beach. Haven't been there since I was about ten and doubt I'll ever be near it again.
You don't know what you're missing.
Oh believe me I do. Sand, lots of it, some with seaweed and dog poo and beyond that icy cold water. No thanks. I take it you have finished your course?
Do I really look that old? Aye I've been working with Grampian Police forensics department for more than a year.
Why did you not go back to Glasgow after you got your degree?
Why would I? I love it up here.
That's good to hear. So you are not one of those weegies who stay on here but bad mouth the city while telling you just how wonderful Glesga is?

Definitely not. Those people really annoy me. There's a girl I know who insists on going back to Glasgow just to get her hair done as if there weren't any decent hairdressers here. Crazy.
So Paula, are you looking forward to next Saturday?
What do you think? The chance to put on a fancy frock and be the centre of attention or at least close to it. That sounds like heaven to me. And I'm really pleased for Lorraine.
Likewise I'm delighted for Kenny. Just glad it's not me.
You mean marrying Lorraine or just getting hitched in general?
Both. But especially the first.
I know you two are not great pals but I'm going to miss Lorraine. We have become really good friends over the course of the last few years. On top of that I can't afford the rental of the flat on my own so now I am going to have to find someone to share it with me.
I'm in exactly the same boat.

About to take another sip of her wine Paula paused when she noticed a smirk on Steven's face.

Don't even think about it!

Lorraine's Dad, who was footing the bill, suggested that they could all walk from Mannofield Church, where the ceremony was to be held, to the Amatola Hotel as it wasn't far and thereby they could cut down on the cost of the fancy cars as they wouldn't have to wait around after they dropped them at the kirk. That was just one of his many money saving suggestions that were quickly quashed by his wife. To be fair to the man he had stepped in when the couple suggested that in their financial situation they would opt for a small and inexpensive affair. Conscious of the fact that Kenny's Mum was a widow he offered to pay for everything; it was at that moment that he gave thanks for the fact that all his other offspring were males.

All Lorraine's fears about having a November wedding proved ill founded. It was mild and sunny and the whole day went like clockwork. The hotel did them proud and Steven was on his best behaviour. His speech was witty and surprisingly respectable and he even included a quote from Shakespeare not because he was a fan of the bard but simply so he could describe the event as being 'Mutch Ado About Nothing'.

The father of the bride gave a warm and emotional speech centring around his beloved daughter while Kenny's nervous efforts were mercifully short and sincere. Having turned down the offer of a room in the hotel, fearful of a late night visit from Steven and the rest of the Stewart Lounge gang, the newlyweds headed for the small flat that they had rented in Esslemont Avenue to spend their first night together; well certainly the first one their parents knew about.

Like every bride's father Billy Hunter had investigated all possible ways of restricting the escalating cost of the wedding but with limited success. He never knew it but he could have enjoyed one minor saving by simply booking one less guest bedroom for the night of the wedding. Individual rooms were reserved for both of the principal attendants and while the best man and the bridesmaid did spend the night at the Amatola, one of their rooms remained totally occupant free.

While the newlywed Mr. And Mrs. Mutch honeymooned in the rather dull surroundings of the Crieff Hydro Steven and Paula were out on the ran-tan night after night. Four weeks later they sat hand in hand on a plane destined for Las Vegas where they frolicked by the swimming pool, gambled modestly and got married.

The wedding was a rather different affair from the recent Aberdeen one. For a start they arrived at the Little White Chapel, a venue totally untainted by class, not in a sedate glorified taxi but in a bright pink Cadillac. The wedding party was also somewhat streamlined in comparison to the 82 people who had witnessed Lorraine and Kenny's nuptials and comprised of a Pastor, who worked in the adjacent used car lot when wedding business was slack, two witnesses brought in for $25 each, and naturally the obligatory Elvis impersonator to serenade them.

No one had a clue what had occurred until they arrived home the following week and broke the news. Lorraine, who had been trying unsuccessfully to contact her pal for days, was obviously astounded and a little hurt that her best pal had kept her in the dark about her plans. She was also horrified when she discovered just who Paula had married and although she tried to keep her concerns from Paula to herself and to display a degree of pleasure, deep down she was convinced that it was nothing more than an aberration on the part of two people who shared a degree of immaturity.

After arriving back in Aberdeen, Steven and Paula had been contemplating what to do with their respective flats now that they were married. Paula was keen on them moving to St Andrews Street while Steven suggested that they set up home on Howburn Place which marked the first of many disagreements. A decision was reached to give up the rental of both and start afresh. Steven as always had grandiose plans and after coming across a very smart property for rent on Queens Road he signed up for a long term lease without even telling the new Mrs. Grant. Seconds out, round two.

Within a matter of a couple of weeks it became clear that the couple would struggle to pay the rental on the posh new abode and still enjoy their mildly pleasure-seeking lifestyle that hadn't diminished in any shape or form despite their new marital status. Although her salary wasn't spectacular Paula loved her job and had no wish to seek out more lucrative employment and made it clear that as it was Steven that had got them into the financial pickle it was up to him to get them out it.

The discovery of oil in the North Sea off the east coast of Scotland had established Aberdeen as the European base of the oil industry and companies flocked to the city to man and service the many oil drilling platforms that had sprung up. Several of Steven's pals had been lured by the wages and could be seen driving around in fancy sports cars and showing

off their Rolex watches. All of which appealed to Steven who had always been attracted by all that glittered.
Initially he assumed that he wouldn't be of any great interest to the oil companies as he doubted if any of the platforms would be looking for a resident DJ but it soon became clear that technical ability wasn't required for many of the more mundane jobs, only a willingness to work and live in harsh conditions for two weeks at a time. Newspapers were full of adverts for roustabout and roughneck jobs that required men to do little more than basic labouring and to keep the rigs tidy and in good working order. He replied to half a dozen of the adverts and within days had half a dozen responses all offering him employment at eye watering rates of pay.
Having had little or no interest in what went on in the North Sea the names meant nothing to Steven but he opted for Mesa Petroleum and the Beatrice oil field. His decision was coloured by two factors. Firstly the Beatrice Alpha platform was a relatively short distance from the Scottish mainland in the Moray Firth and consequently somewhat more sheltered from the worst of the weather conditions. Secondly he once had a brief but passionate affair with a French girl called Beatrice of who he still had fond memories.
He was a little reticent to break the news of his decision to Paula. After all they had only been married for a few months and he assumed she would be upset by the fact that he would be working a two weeks on, two weeks off rota. He needn't have worried as Paula was thrilled after he revealed how much he would be earning and thought of all the things they could now afford such as a decent car and foreign holidays.

Although relieved that she took it so well, Steven was a little bit hurt that she was so at ease with him being absent half of every month.
His life choice didn't go down so well with his mother and father who were horrified and he could just imagine them making up some story to relate to their dinner party friends *Oh Steven has got himself this very well paid job working abroad.* His mother had previously refused to tell anyone that he was a DJ preferring *Steven is working in the music industry.*
After going through the safety courses Steven suddenly found himself on a helicopter heading for the platform and the start of a new chapter and he quickly discovered that life on the platform wasn't half as bad as he had feared. Okay the work was hard and cold and repetitive but he enjoyed the meals prepared by top chefs and, being a film buff, loved the fact there was a cinema room. While many of his fellow workers would only frequent the facility if the movie being shown couldn't be seen in the local Odeon and featured a cast of people chosen for their physique rather than their acting ability, Steven was delighted to watch everything on show with a particular love of art house films. When these involved subtitles he usually found that he had the place to himself.
After two weeks of starring at nothing but the cold North Sea Steven couldn't wait to get home to his posh West End pad and his waiting wife. Despite what writers of crime fiction might suggest the local Police force in cities with a population of quarter of a million are not confronted with a murder twice every week and most Sundays and when the body of a young

German hitchhiker was discovered in woodland on the outskirts of Aberdeen Grampian Police soon had a case on their hands that attracted considerable media attention.
Under pressure to find a culprit, leave was cancelled and overtime in all departments became the norm and Steven discovered that he was seeing considerably less of his new missus than he had hoped. With most of his regular mates at work during the day Steven began gravitating towards the Dutch Mill pub and drinking sessions with other refugees from the platforms and rigs. Before he knew it the two weeks at home had gone along with a substantial proportion of the money he had earned and it was time to head for the Heliport again.
In that way a pattern quickly emerged and when the pressure of work had diminished, Paula hoped that the couple could restore some sort of social life during the time when Steven was onshore. Unfortunately by then he had got into a pattern of spending his afternoons downing pints of lager and he normally arrived home with no ambition to do anything more than fall asleep in front of the television much to Paula's chagrin and frustration.
The Police service has never been populated with people who gravitated towards abstinence and local hostelries benefitted greatly from the support of members of Aberdeen's finest. Paula had generally turned down invites to *come and join me for a swift half* usually emanating from a male co-worker with a wife waiting at home with a posse of his kids. But bored out of her mind when Steven was offshore and only mildly

happier when he was home she began to go along to the cop after-hour gatherings.
The group varied from night to night depending who was on duty but gradually it began to dawn on her that Donnie, a middle aged Detective Sergeant, was not only there every time she went along but always seemed to manoeuvre so that he was her bosom buddy. Literally. It was after a particularly heavy night when the squad were celebrating putting 'a villain' they had been after a long time behind bars that Donnie suggested that they share a taxi as they were *headed in the same direction.* It was only as they approached Paula's home that she established that he in fact stayed in Cove Bay.
She subsequently blamed her level of inebriation for her decision to allow Donnie to pay off the taxi and join her for night cap but she knew that the drink was only one factor and that loneliness played a far bigger role. Whatever the reason, she shared a bowl of Cornflakes with him the next morning.
After a few weeks, Donnie began to trot out a few stock phrases about his wife not understanding him and how he was only staying with her for the kids. Much to Paula's surprise, however, he did leave the marital home and get himself a small flat in the far from salubrious King Street which had the joint advantages of being inexpensive and close to his place of work.

By the time he had completed his sixth stint on the platform Steven was wearying of the life style. He had watched all the movies at least twice and had eaten more T-bone steaks than the average Texas ranch owner. He was also well aware that the relationship with Paula was decidedly rocky and made up his mind that when he got home he would sit down with her to discuss the future. To see if there was any way they could cut their cloth so that it might be possible for him to find a job where he wouldn't have to spend half of his life offshore.

When he entered the flat he instantly knew something was wrong as the place had an empty feel about it. He hadn't necessarily expected to find Paula there on a weekday afternoon but there was more to it than that. The house was cold and felt like it hadn't been lived in for ages. It was when he entered their bedroom to dump his bag that he immediately knew something was amiss. The room was neat. None of the clothes Paula had worn the previous day were scattered around the floor and the dressing table wasn't littered with make-up and perfume bottles. It was, however, when he looked inside the wardrobe that it all became crystal clear; there wasn't a stitch of his wife's clothing hanging there.

He found the letter in the lounge. It was short and to the point; the marriage wasn't working and she was off and wouldn't be coming back. Although they had been married less than a year he knew Paula well enough to realise that once she made up her mind that hell would freeze over before she changed it. So his initial idea of going down to Police HQ to have it out with her was quickly shelved. Like it or not, and he didn't like it, he was more or less single again.

In one of his rash moments, not his first and certainly not his last, he had signed for the flat in his name only although they had always shared the rent. But since Mrs. Grant would no longer be living there it became obvious that Mrs. Grant would no longer be contributing and that Steven would be solely responsible for its upkeep. The lease had more than a year to run and Steven realised that he would struggle to keep paying the rental from any onshore job he could get and that he had no option but to head back. And in best Steven Grant style he faced adversity in the only way that he knew how to by spending money as he headed for the John Clark's car showroom on the corner of Holburn Street he had passed so many times. But this time he wasn't like a kid starring in through a toy shop window as he marched inside and signed an HP agreement for a brand new BMW 320i, red with cream leather upholstery naturally.

Lorraine was saddened when she met Paula for a coffee and heard what had happened. Saddened but certainly not surprised. If Ladbrokes had been offering odds on the marriage not lasting more than a year she would have had a little flutter and would have ended up financially better off.

CHAPTER ELEVEN

After their weddings Steven and Kenny saw less of each other although the Saturday routine was still adhered to. But then Steven went offshore and the best pals drifted further apart. Kenny did meet up with Steven and his newly acquired mates in the Dutch Mill, their chosen watering hole, when he was onshore but he couldn't keep up with them either in consumption or financially as the oil rich brigade flashed wads of notes. After the second session when Kenny arrived home slightly worse for wear and substantially poorer he always made an excuse when Steven suggested meeting there. In truth life had changed for Kenny when he got wed and he was more than content to spend time in their cosy flat. Unlike the turbulent year the Grants had suffered, Kenny and Lorraine settled quickly into married life although not surprisingly it had its ups and downs. Three days after returning from their short honeymoon he found Lorraine in tears. Like all men he assumed that he had done something wrong but after racking his brain couldn't for the life of him work out exactly what it was. Eventually she explained that she simply missed her Mum which made no sense to Kenny as she hadn't lived with her for some time prior to the wedding but knew better to say anything to that effect, merely assuring her that all would be well. And it was.

The flat they were renting suited them perfectly. Being in the Rosemount area there were a plethora of small shops on their doorstep and yet it was a comfortable ten minute stroll to

Union Street, Aberdeen's main thoroughfare. With a decent sized lounge with a gas fire, a snug bedroom, a small but adequate kitchen and a bathroom it was all that a young couple could possibly need and they were totally contented with their lot.

Days after they had celebrated their first anniversary in a modest but pleasing manner with a meal, set out on their drop leaf table in front of the fire, of a Chinese carry out and a bottle of Asti Spumante which Kenny largely consumed on his own, Lorraine broke the news. She was pregnant. Kenny was ecstatic at the thought of being a Dad and Lorraine's parents were also happy although the fact this would be their fourth grandchild perhaps diluted their excitement a little. On the other hand for Kenny's Mum this would be her first and she was so thrilled that she didn't even phone her sister or her cousin but instead visited them so she could see their faces when she imparted the news.

From that moment Kenny's attitude to Lorraine changed and he began to treat her like a porcelain doll. He asked her if she was feeling alright ten times a day and ran after her morning, noon and night. He wouldn't even let her carry a bag of shopping up the stairs and by the time she was six months pregnant she was growing so weary of his well meaning but overbearing attention that she even spoke to her mother about it. Marilyn just laughed and told her to make the best of it on the grounds that it would only happen with the first born.

Lorraine enjoyed a relatively trouble free nine months and within four hours of arriving at the Maternity Hospital she gave birth to the seven pound six ounce Alison Jane Mutch. Kenny was on cloud nine for close on two days until he began to worry about all the things that could go wrong and the immense responsibility of having to care for such a helpless little creature. He also quickly discovered that the same helpless little creature could scream in a manner that must have startled everyone living within a quarter of a mile radius of their flat with the decibel level seeming to increase further by several notches in the early hours of each morning.

When the wee one arrived Steven was offshore but told Kenny that he wanted to meet up as soon as he got back. Although Steven had always made it clear that he had no interest in ever having kids of his own he was genuinely pleased for his pal as he knew that Kenny would make a great father. It was on the day that Alison celebrated her one week birthday, seven days that felt like seven months to her sleep deprived parents, that Kenny wandered into the Stewart Lounge and found not only his mate waiting for him but an equally welcome pint of Tennant's and a very large whisky.

Oh here's Daddy. Has anyone told you that you look terrible?
Nae need. I hiv' looked in the mirror.
Anyway. Congratulations and drink up.
I hope that there's waater in this.
Aye. A wee drop. So how is the wee lass?
Thriving but noisy.
So that's why you look like you haven't slept in a week?

No I look like I hinna slept in a wik because I hinna slept in a wik. Naebody warns you how hard it's gaen to be. But worth it, jist to see the wee thing sleepin' peacefully. The odd hour she dis sleep.
And she's called Alison?
Alison Jane. Named aifter Lorraine's twa Grunnies.
I am so relieved that it wasn't a boy.
Why?
Because knowing you and your obsession with a certain football team I could just imagine the lad being lumbered with a name like Miller Mutch.
Rubbish. It wis gaen to be Rougvie Mutch!
How are you managing for space? You've just got the one bedroom.
It's nae a problem at the moment. We need to hae her beside us onywiy so we have the cot alangside oor bed. Aye Lorraine's side of the bed! But lang term we will hae to look for a place with twa bedrooms. There's a few roon aboot us and we like that area so we'll be fine.
Never thought about buying a place of your own.
Oh I'd like tae. But wi' jist the one wage comin' in now we couldnae afford it. Certainly nae on Asda wages.
Now don't start complaining about money just because it's your round.
Okay but this is my last. I've got tae get up the road aifter this.
Already?
Aye for the bath.

Oh is this you and Lorraine sharing an evening amidst the bubbles.
I wish. Nae it's the wee one that needs her bath and Lorraine likes me to help.
Okay but I hope you aren't going to be such a lightweight at the head wetting.
Aboot that Steven...
Don't even think about backing out. It's all arranged.

Kenny had never been a great drinker certainly not in comparison to his fellow Stewart Lounge regulars. After his stag party he had been bedded for twenty four hours with a basin beside his bed and he wasn't looking forward to a repeat performance. But it was a tradition and he would just have to get on with it and he survived, in truth rather enjoying a break from the domesticity and later sleeping like a log thanks to the copious quantities of alcohol he had consumed.
Alison Jane thrived and flourished much to the delight and surprise of her father who would scuttle to find his mother's old medical book to read about pneumonia and diphtheria and a hundred rare diseases, many never found beyond the shores of Africa, every time the girl would sneeze or cough. It was when she was eight months old that the couple both concluded that it would be nice to be able to sleep in a bedroom of their own without waking regularly to check that their daughter was alright.
After a lengthy discussion Kenny began to check out available two bedroom flats that fitted within their limited budget. He found one in Northfield Place which was still within their

preferred Rosemount area; only minor disadvantage was that the landlord wanted a long term lease although Kenny didn't envisage that as a major problem until he began speaking to Lorraine about it. It was then that she revealed that she had just heard from the doctor who confirmed that the family of three would soon be a foursome.

They talked long into the night and reluctantly concluded that they shouldn't commit themselves to the rental of another property until they saw how things turned out. If it was another girl then a two bedroom flat would probably do them certainly in the short term although Kenny eventually wanted to provide a house with a garden for his kids. On the other hand if the new little Mutch was a boy then ideally they would need a three bedroom house.

The assistant manager at the Asda superstore was due to retire and Kenny had toyed with the idea of applying for the job which would mean a substantial increase in salary to a level that would allow the couple to afford a mortgage on a modest home of their own. Kenny had been reluctant about putting his name forward as although the position was better paid it brought with it a great deal more responsibility but in the light of Lorraine's news he decided to at least investigate further.

Since the day that Kenny first began stacking shelves at the store he had worked under general manager Hugh Stewart and had always got on well with the stern but fair man. He requested a meeting and asked for his boss's advice which was simply *go for it Kenny.* He also informed Kenny that while the decision would ultimately be made at head office he would certainly provide a very favourable letter of recommendation. On that basis Kenny went ahead and was quietly confident that with his unblemished record of employment that he had a pretty good chance of securing the position.

Lorraine was so convinced of his success that she began house hunting or rather studying brochures of new homes being built in the rapidly expanding Bridge of Don suburb. The scheme being dcveloped by a well known local builder largely comprised of small semis with fairly basic facilities but all did boast a postage stamp garden and most importantly three bedrooms even if one of them would barely allow them to spin a feline if they ever added such a creature to their expanding family.

Having spent many hours assessing their finances they concluded that with Kenny's increased salary they could afford the mortgage and they put down a small deposit so that they got the partially built home on the corner plot they both fancied. It was basically full speed ahead until Kenny received a summons up to Hugh's office where a clearly disappointed and slightly embarrassed boss man conveyed the news that HQ had opted to move the manager of a small Asda store in Yorkshire to Aberdeen to take up the post.

Kenny was shattered and kept the news to himself for days, feeling a failure and just too disappointed to tell his wife. On a day off he contacted Steven simply because he needed to speak to someone.

Hi mate. Sorry to hear your news. They must be mad to pass over someone as reliable and conscientious as you.

Peety you hidnae been on the selection committee then.
Bet there wasn't even a committee. Where's the guy coming from?
Somewhere in Yorkshire.
And where's Asda's head office?
Leeds.
Exactly! Old pals act. Time for you to move on I think.
To where? If I canna get a job there what chunce hiv I got onywiy else?
Then perhaps the time has come for a radical change. What's Lorraine saying about it?
I hinna telt her yet.
What!
I ken she'll be so disappinted and I feel like I'm lettin' her doon.
That's rubbish. It's not your fault.
But we hid everythin' planned oot. Even pit doon a deposit on a hoose in Bridge of Don.
How much?
It's only £250 but it's the principle. Lorraine hid already started thinking about carpets and curtains and the like.
Then as I said, think of doing something else.
Like fit?
Why not come offshore with me.
Can you really see me as a roustabout?
With your puny physique, no. But there's other jobs. You know I'm on the Piper Alpha now?
Aye. How is it?

Not a lot different from the previous platform but at least it's a changed view of the North Sea and they've got a few films I haven't seen before. Anyway they are always looking for catering staff and with your experience in the bakery department at Asda I reckon they would welcome you with open arms. And the money is great. Certainly more than enough to afford a semi in Bridge of Don.
I ken it makes sense but...
In your case it certainly does. By the time I have been home for two weeks all the money is gone but I know you would be frugal and stay out of the pubs.
Aye I wid but...no, I wid miss Lorraine and wee Alison too much. I wid hate nae to see her growin' up.
If you played your cards right you could make enough in a year or so that you would be set for life and when you were offshore you could be looking out for a decent paid onshore job. And you would still have two weeks out of every four that you would be with them, twenty four hours a day, no evening working or weekends apart. And by the time you have spent a fortnight with a bairn, two of them soon, you will be desperate to get back to the platform.
No way!
I know I would.
But how wid I convince Lorraine?
Whoa. You're on your own there son.
You dinna want to come up the road wi' me and help me tae sell the idea tae her dae you?
I'd rather go to a Daniel O'Donnell concert.

It was several days later before Kenny plucked up the courage to broach the subject with Lorraine. He waited until a Friday when Alison had been behaving reasonably well. He ran a bath for Lorraine and prepared a fancy meal he had brought home. It was after he had downed his second glass of wine that he launched into a prepared spiel.

I didnae get the job at Asda.
You're joking!
Afraid not.
So who did?
They're bringing someone up from Yorkshire.
That's not fair.
I agree. And so dis Hugh but it wis a heid office decision.
Stinks of cronyism to my mind.
I agree but well...
Kenny what are we going to do about the house?
I hiv got a plan. Well it wis mair o' Steven's plan to be truthful.
You told him before you told me?
I've bin meanin' tae tell you for days but...I couldnae face disappinting you. I feel such a failure.
Rubbish. It is clearly internal politics. So come on what's the plan although with Steven involved I am not sure I want to hear it?
Steven is suggestin' that I ging offshore.
What!
Jist for a short time.
Kenny you're not built for manual work.

Oh I ken, dinna worry. He thinks that the caterin' company on the rig he is workin' on now are lookin' for staff and he reckons that wi' my experience at Asda I'd get a job.
And leave me here with a baby and toddler to look after?
It wid only be twa wiks oot o' fower. And your Mither would help I'm sure. She did that wi' yer brither's kids. And my Ma wid be delighted to come through and spend some time wi' her grandkids. And then I wid be here ivery day for a fortnicht.
You would hate it.
Absolutely. I ken I wid but we wid set a time limit. Nae mair than a year, hopefully less. The money their payin' is amazin'. In nae time we could afford the full deposit on the new hoose, set up the mortgage and furnish it and then I could look oot for a better peyed job onshore.
And if you didnae finds one?
Then I wid find a job of some kind and with the help of the Grunnies you could ging back to work.
Oh great!
I'm sure it winna come to that. Steven says that I wid be workin' wi' top chefs and wi' that experience I'm sure I could get something worthwhile back here. It's the only wiy we'll ever be able to get a hoose o' oor ain.
Aye I suppose your right.
Let's sleep on it and see if the idea appeals ony mair in the mornin'

The following morning did bring a change in attitudes. Lorraine, visualising her smart brand new house, had rather warmed to the idea while Kenny on the other hand had begun to get cold feet. But he knew it was the correct thing to do even if he dreaded the thought of life on an oil platform.

CHAPTER TWELVE

Kenny was nervous as he arrived at the palatial offices of ARA, or Aberdeen Recruitment Agency, on Rubislaw Terrace but was met by a charming, and rather attractive, girl called Amy who not only instantly provided him with a coffee but also quickly put him at ease. He had submitted his CV to the company a week earlier explaining that he wanted to work on Piper Alpha and had been asked to attend for an interview.
The night prior to the interview he had spent hours practicing replies to a host of question he suspected he would be asked. After a few minutes of small talk, however, Amy asked him only one simple question – *when can you start?* He confirmed that he could begin work soon but would need to check the notice period for his present employment, which proved to be four weeks. But he also wanted to try and synchronize with Steven so that he would enjoy the benefit of a friendly face on the platform and possibly even a shoulder to cry on when he took this giant step into the unknown.
Subsequently a date six weeks after the initial interview was agreed on and he was able to work at Asda until the very day before he was due to leave home. That meant that there wouldn't be any period without wages coming in and also that he didn't spend a couple of weeks at home sitting brooding. Being both a popular and relatively long term member of staff, he was given a small leaving party with a cake that Kenny had actually baked himself. His boss at Asda was

genuinely sad to see him go and provided him with a glowing reference which he felt sure would help him when he began his search for employment back on the safety of dry land.
Then suddenly the reality began to sink in. The reality that when he went to bed the next night he wouldn't be snuggling up to his wife or giving his adorable little one a goodnight kiss and if there had been any way to avoid leaving the next day Kenny would have grabbed it with both hands. But the die was cast and he had no option but to get on with it.

Hurrying out the door the next morning with only a cursory farewell to his girls in case he broke down he found Steven waiting for him alongside a taxi.

What's with the long face?
Fit do you think?
You'll be fine.
I dinna ken how I let you talk me intae this.
As I remember it you didn't take a lot of persuading. The idea of the fat wage packet and the house of your own were all that it took. Anyway let's go. We don't want to miss the helicopter.
Oh dinna mention it!
The flight will be fine. Sometimes it can be a bit bumpy but there's hardly any wind today.
Steven, I once felt sick comin' doon in the lift in St. Nicholas Hoose.
You'll be fine.
Aye so you keep sayin'

And if you don't like it when you get there you can always come home tomorrow.
Really?
No, of course not. I just said that to try to cheer you up.
Well you hinna succeeded.
Stop worrying mate. I'll be there to look after you.
Promise?
Yes I promise.

As his experience of being in airports was restricted to Aberdeen, which he found pokey and rather dated, and Alicante Kenny was taken aback by how vibrant and busy the heliport at Dyce was. Rows of brightly coloured helicopters in the livery of Bristows and British Airways stood side by side and men carrying the obligatory duffle bag swarmed towards the waiting fleet or hurried away from a chopper, looking for a taxi that would no doubt ferry them as quickly as possible to the nearest pub after two weeks of abstention. Steven, chatting nonstop to try to keep his pal's spirits up, explained that he was about to take off from the busiest heliport in the world. Kenny looked suitably unimpressed.

Kenny had prepared himself for the worst which was just as well as he was sick several times on the trip out leaving Steven to wonder how he would get on when they flew on a real North East winter's day. When he wasn't throwing up Kenny studied the other men on the flight with him and was surprised at just how old many of them were. He had assumed they would all be in their twenties and thirties but that wasn't the case and he wondered what attracted older men, some of whom looked like they might be nearing retirement age, to spend their lives on an isolated oil platform. After a few weeks as he got to know them he realised that many were just like him; willing to put up with the hardship and the loneliness simply to help their families enjoy a better standard of life. Ordinary hard working lads with whom he quickly bonded.

At the start, however, he found Piper Alpha a bit of a culture shock and he hated the dirt and the grime and the constant noise of the drilling equipment twenty four hours a day. Steven had explained to Kenny that the cabins were jointly occupied but conveniently omitted to mention the fact that the bunk beds were also shared with men on the alternate shift. It meant that the bedding was always warm but Kenny was far from impressed with the fact that he appeared to be sharing a bed with someone who didn't even have a passing acquaintance with Right Guard. For the first few days he was totally miserable and convinced that once he got home he would never return. But slowly he began to get used to the life.

The canteen was on the top floor of the platform just below the helideck and Kenny was pleasantly surprised by it. It wasn't quite the dining room of the Marcliffe Hotel but it was clean and surprisingly cheerful and he thought the tartan curtains on the windows and the rows of potted plants were a nice homely touch. Despite the fact that life in the kitchens was incredibly intense and hard work and seemed to comprise of rushing about in a room with a strong resemblance to a sauna while being shouted out by men with a seemingly limited vocabulary he got used to it. Quite quickly the senior chefs realised that Kenny was a dedicated and dependable member of the team and began to entrust him with more and more responsibility. Kenny loved learning from chefs of real talent and the long and arduous days had one great advantage; it meant that he was so dog tired after a twelve hour shift that he slept like a log despite the unfortunate smell emanating from the bed.

After four spells on Piper Alpha Kenny enjoyed the reward that his commitment and selflessness deserved; the keys to their own house on Jesmond Drive. As it was the couple's first real home he insisted on carrying Lorraine across the threshold, despite her greatly expanded waistline, much to her amusement. For the first few days of his two weeks off he did nothing but revel in the joy in ownership of what to him was a luxurious property and with the May weather being benign spent hour after hour just soaking up the rays in the wee back garden.

But during his second week at home he left his little piece of Utopia to visit Amy at ARA, who had left a message that she would like to see him. When he arrived at the Recruitment Company's office Amy explained that the catering contract on Piper Alpha was being taken over in a couple of months by a different company and that they were on the lookout for staff. Kenny confirmed that he was happy to work for anyone as long as it was on the same rig and that the pay wasn't any less.

Before he went to see Amy he had further amended his CV to take account of the talents he had acquired during his brief spell offshore and added a copy of a letter from the head chef on Piper Alpha, a well known figure in catering circles, praising Kenny in quite glowing terms.
Amy agreed to look around to see if something suitable was available but the next time Kenny set off on that dreaded helicopter he had heard nothing further from her and wondered if all her positive words were simply to ensure that he didn't take his business elsewhere. But then two days after coming back to Aberdeen the telephone rang.

Hi, is that Kenny?
Aye.
Kenny, its Amy at ARA. How are things?
Oh a'right, Enjoying being hame.
Anyway Kenny, I may just have something that would suit you.
Really?
Yes but there is a catch. The vacancy won't arise until September.
That's okay. Tell me mair.
It's with a very well known and highly regarded local hotel and wedding venue. They will be looking for a pastry chef but also someone who can stand in if the sous chef is working at another establishment the company own. Do you think you could cope with that?
Definitely.
The money is good. Not offshore levels obviously but decent. Do you want me to try and fix up an interview for you?

Most definitely.
Okay leave it with me.

He said nothing that day to Lorraine in case it all fell through and was thrilled when his new best pal Amy called back with the news that they were interested in him. He met with the general manager and the existing pastry chef, an ebullient elderly gentleman who explained that he had worked in kitchens for well over forty years and had decided that the time had come to retire. The hotel company had, however, persuaded him to stay on until mid September by which time the summer holiday trade would be slowing down and which would also provide time for a new man to get settled in before the festive period. The head chef had apparently been due to sit in on the meeting but at the last minute had declared that he was *just too busy* signalling that if he got the job Kenny would be working with another temperamental chef. As if there were any other kind.
When asked why he had decided to work offshore Kenny answered with his usual honesty admitting to the fact that he hated being away from home for long periods but that he was willing to make the sacrifice so that his wife and daughter could enjoy a better quality of life. Both men were clearly impressed by the young lad as became clear the following day.

Kenny, its Amy. They want to offer you the job.
What? I thought I hid nae chunce.

Well I did wonder if your lack of experience would count against you but they explained that they were so impressed by you as a person that they were willing to take a chance. But...
Aye I thoucht there wid be a 'but'.
It is only that they want to offer you a three month trial period starting 1 October. Would you be happy with that?
Of course. I'm nae feart of bein' on trial. I've daen that afore. I winna let you doon Amy.
I'm sure you won't. I think they have already made you aware of the salary.
Aye and of the Christmas bonus! As you said it is naethin' like offshore wages but we can manage fine on that. And I wid be able to ging to my work on a bus nae that affa helicopter.

At the end of June Kenny was stepping on board that 'affa helicopter' safe in the knowledge that in less than three months he would never, ever have to get on one again.

CHAPTER THIRTEEN

Kenny never found out how he managed to wangle it but Steven was always able to ensure that they shared a cabin and during the late evening of Wednesday 6h July 1988 Kenny and Steven lay quietly on their respective bunks. Kenny had completed a twelve hour shift that had begun at six that morning but was having difficulty in drifting off to sleep despite the fact that the alarm was set for 5.30 the next morning. Steven was knocking in time until he began the dreaded midnight shift. He had thought about going to the cinema but they were showing *Caddyshack* and he had already seen it. Twice. And while it was funny it wasn't THAT funny that he could sit through it again.

As a result the two men passed the time by reading although their literary tastes were somewhat different. Kenny was engrossed with a Booker prize winning novel while Steven's choice had considerably less words but an abundance of coloured glossy photographs largely of women with a remarkable absence of apparel.

Bored, Steven decided to try and engage his roommate in conversation.

What are you reading Kenny?
It's a book called 'Moon Tiger'.
Weird title.
It won the Booker Prize last year.

Oh aye. What's it about?
It's aboot a wifie lyin' in a hospital bed in London and lookin' back on her life.
Wow. Sounds like barrel of laughs.
I'll gie you a read o' it fan I'm finished if you like.
Thanks all the same but I think I will stick to my 'Razzle'.

Just at that moment there was a loud explosion, so severe that it shook the cups and glasses in their cabin.

Fit the hell wis that?
I don't know.
I better go and find oot fit's happenin'.

Kenny swung down from the top bunk he had been occupying and left the cabin to be met by a waft of smoke and instantly became aware of flames shooting high into the air on the other side of the platform. He rushed back to alert Steven.

Steven! The platform's on fire!
Don't worry. The fire crew will sort it out. There's always something like this happening on Piper Alpha but the emergency guys quickly get things under control. They'll sort it.

Just as Steven was about to resume browsing through his magazine the lights went out and in the darkness both men become conscious of the sounds of the some of their fellow workmen running around and shouting in a clearly distressed manner. At that point Steven thought that perhaps he should check things out for himself and when he got out onto the deck he was suddenly less blasé about the situation as some of the nonchalance he had felt began to dissipate. There was mayhem and sheer blind panic amongst the men who were milling about and who had realised that this wasn't just 'another incident' but something far, far more serious. Steven stood frozen to the spot totally unable to think of what to do but Kenny quickly realised the dangers that might lie ahead and rushed back into the cabin, remerging with two towels he had soaked in water which they then wound round their faces.

Kenny, you read the safety booklets didn't you?
Aye.
What is it we are supposed to do?
Eventually get to the helideck.
That's a waste of time. Helicopters won't be able to land with the flames and the smoke.
Onywiy, the first thing we're supposed tae dae is tae get to the muster station so let's dae that.
Where's the muster station?
Beside one of the lifeboats on the next level up.
Right, let's go.

The two men headed for the stairway leading to the appropriate lifeboat station but before they could reach it they encountered a row of men stumbling through the smoke each one holding onto the shoulder of the man in front. The men had towels wrapped round their mouths and even their eyes

and Kenny thought it resembled old films from the First World War showing images of soldiers who had been gassed. It was a scene of total horror and increased Steven and Kenny's awareness of the urgent need to get off the platform. However as soon as they reached the stairway they discovered that wasn't going to be easy as due to the fire and the smoke the stairway was totally impassable.
Desperately seeking an alternate route Steven spotted a metal ladder and without thinking began to climb it. The screams he emitted coupled with a colourful stream of oaths must have been heard some distance away. It was only when he had grabbed the bottom rung that Steven realised that the ladder was red hot instantly burning the skin of both of his hands. Once he stopped cursing he began to focus on the task facing them with the need for a quick decision becoming increasingly more obvious as another huge explosion rocked the platform.

Well it looks like we can't go up pal so there is only one other direction we can go. Down.
But the security manuals a' state that we hiv tae go tae the muster station.
I think they were written for something considerably less serious than this. To be honest I doubt there's ever being anything like this before. Anywhere.
Okay. But if we are going doon tae the sea we should hiv put on our lifejackets.
True. I'll go back to cabin for them.

No dinna bother Steven. There's a store room I wis in the ither day near here and there were spares hinging there. I'll get them.

Despite the poor visibility caused by the clouds of smoke Kenny succeeded in reaching the store and found not only life jackets but heavy duty powerful torches.

Good lad. But why did you take half a dozen jackets?
Tae gie to some o' the ither lads, the ones I have bin workin' wi' in the kitchen recently, if I can find them and they need life jackets.
We don't have time to go looking for other folk Kenny. We have got to get ourselves off.
We'll jist hiv to mak' time.
Don't be stupid. In a situation like this it is every man for himself.
Sorry Steven, I couldnae live wi' maesel if I didnae at least try.
You're a right stubborn brute.
Aye, I ken
I'll go and see if I can find the best way to get further down and I'll meet you back at this exact spot in ten minutes. Ten minutes and not a minute longer.

While Kenny headed off in one direction trudging through the gloom, burdened down by armfuls of life jackets, Steven headed off the opposite way. Steven hadn't gone more than a few yards when he became aware of a fellow worker perched

on the edge of the platform staring into the abyss below. It became clear to Steven that the guy was building up the courage to jump despite the fact that they were on a deck high above the sea and that large patches of the water were ablaze as a result of spillages of oil. Only then did he truly realise how serious the situation was; if someone was contemplating taking such dangerous and dramatic action he wondered if there would come a moment when he would have to make the same decision. Steven had never paid too much attention to safety briefings but he did remember one occasion when it had been explained to them that jumping into the sea from a height of 30ft could prove fatal. If he couldn't find any way of getting further down the platform he was looking at a drop from a deck 68ft above sea level.
Undaunted he trudged on desperately looking for a stairway that would take them down towards the sea and provide a potential means for escape but without success, arriving at the South East corner only to discover that there wasn't a stairway as he had hoped there would be. He turned and began to return to the point where he had split up from Kenny when suddenly the torch light revealed a rope hanging over the side and although it was difficult to see in the gloom, it appeared to stretch down to the sea. It wasn't a perfect scenario by any means but beggars couldn't be choosers.
He decided to go back to tell Kenny although he was far from convinced that Kenny, who he always described as a bit of a feartie, would even consider scaling down that rope. In any event when he got back to the point near the accommodation cabins where the two men had parted there was no sign of

Kenny or anyone else for that matter. He checked his watch and found that more than ten minutes had expired since they separated. Perhaps Kenny had come back to find that Steven wasn't there and headed off with some of his mates from the kitchens. After all Steven had been clear that they were to meet up in ten minutes and no longer. Steven thought about going off to try and locate him but as the conditions were getting worse by the minute, with the flames creeping closer and the smoke getting thicker by the second, he realised that the chance of finding him was remote. So what were the alternatives? He had told Kenny that it was every man for himself and Steven reluctantly acted on that premise and returned to the rope he had found.

Having been once bitten, or in Steven's case once burned, he should have been twice shy but in those desperate minutes he wasn't thinking clearly and he simply grabbed for the rope oblivious to the possibility that it might be too hot to hold onto with hands that had recently been deprived of their skin. On this occasion he didn't even have time to seek out a few appropriate oaths as he let go of the rope and suddenly found himself plunging though the darkness towards the sea below.

He hit the water with such force that he was totally winded and left without the energy to force his way to the surface. At that moment in time he gave a silent thank you to Kenny for his foresight in locating a life jacket. He also gave thanks to a deity he had never believed in for the fact that he had landed in a patch of the sea that wasn't ablaze with burning oil.

Quite rapidly his relief turned to concern as he realised that he was in the waters of the North Sea and although it was July the water temperature was still only about 12 degrees and with no survival suit on hypothermia would set in quickly. Fortunately a damaged lifeboat which had been blown off the platform by one of the explosions was floating nearby and he was sufficiently energised by its discovery that he was able to swim to it. His efforts to clamber aboard were, however, proving futile until two pairs of hands suddenly appeared from the vessel and pulled him out of the water. The blackened and weary faces of the two oil workers was one of the most gratifying and welcoming sights of his entire life.

The next thirty minutes passed in a blur as he drifted in and out of consciousness until suddenly he found himself being gently lifted out of the lifeboat and on to a small FCR, a fast rescue craft, which in turn transported him to the *Silver Pit,* a converted trawler being utilised as a support vessel for the Piper and Claymore fields and which had fortunately been close by the stricken platform. His hands were salved and bandaged and a thick and warm grey blanket placed round his shoulders before he was presented with the most welcome cup of tea he had ever tasted.

Steven sat on the deck of the boat with several other survivors in varied states of shock with some of them having clearly suffered far more serious injuries than he had sustained. No one spoke because there was simply nothing to say; they all just stared at the blazing platform in disbelief. To a film buff like Steven it was like watching the *Towering Inferno,* his favourite disaster movie, except that the men dying or jumping into the fiery sea in a desperate attempt to escape weren't actors who would go home at night with a fat pay

check. They were decent honest men, many of whom he had got to know personally, who seemed in danger of sacrificing their lives for the black gold.
Amongst them was his best pal, a man he had faithfully promised to look after, a man he felt he had deserted in his hour of greatest need. And as he sat on that deck tears smeared his smoke stained face.

The moment that Steven moved away, Kenny began his hunt for his kitchen pals several of whom had clocked off with him a mere four hours ago but in some ways light years earlier. Most of them he had only known for a week but on a platform when you work and live in such close contact friendships are quickly formed.
He knew the area of the accommodation that they were in and headed straight for it. As he pushed open the door to the first cabin he was suddenly totally engulfed in thick acrid smoke which was burning his eyes and his throat and making it difficult to breath. Even the heavy duty torch he had found did nothing to cut through the gloom and all he could do was shout out. When there was no reply he assumed that the cabin was empty and moved onto the next one with the same negative result.
Kenny was carefully watching the time to ensure that he didn't miss the link up with Steven and so he decided to give it only one more try. The third cabin was equally smoke filled but on this occasion his shout was met by a response. A faint response but a call for help nevertheless, delivered in a thick Newcastle accent that Kenny instantly recognised.

Is that you Bobby?
Aye man, it's me.
It's Kenny. You've got to get out of here.
I canny man. Something fell on me leg and I canny move.
Bobby, just keep speaking so I can find you.

Guided by words from the Geordie tongue Kenny edged his way across the floor to the far side of the cabin where he found his pal from the kitchens and discovered that a metal locker had toppled over, landing on the man's leg and in all probability fracturing it in the process. Kenny's breathing was becoming more and more difficult as a consequence of smoke inhalation but summoning all his strength he managed to lift the locker off Bobby.

Bobby, put your airm roon my shoulders and I'll see if I canna get you oot of this place. It's nae that much better outside but at least there is some fresh air.

Kenny honestly didn't know what he was going to do with the man who appeared to be in great distress once he got him out of the cabin but all he knew was that he couldn't just leave him there to die. The biggest problem was that in the dark Kenny had become totally disoriented and he had no idea where the door was. Supporting Bobby as best he could he inched his way along one wall in the hope that he was going towards the exit and not further into the room but gradually what remained of his strength ebbed away and his movement became more laboured with each step.

Bobby I'm gaen tae hae to stop for a minute lad. I'm knackered.
Aye. You should have tried to rescue someone no as fat as me man.

Despite the predicament they were in Kenny laughed as he gently lowered his workmate to the floor before sliding down the wall to sit beside him.

Jist gie me a couple o' minutes 'til I get my breath back and we'll gie it anither try.

Kenny didn't know it at the time but those were the last words he would ever utter as the smoke overcame him and he slowly descended in unconsciousness not realising that he was in fact within six inches of the door to the cabin and to possible salvation.

CHAPTER FOURTEEN

For years after the events of 1988 if anyone who had been in Aberdeen on the night of 6/7th July was asked what they remembered most about Piper Alpha the answer would always be 'the helicopters'. Back then the rather parochial Aberdeen Airport closed at 9.30 every evening which led to a great deal of frustration with travellers using the facility. If you were on a plane flying to the city during the late evening and it was delayed for whatever reason you could find yourself being diverted to Edinburgh Airport with the attraction of then being ferried by coach the one hundred plus miles north.
The sound of air traffic in the early hours of Thursday 7th July therefore roused many people from their slumbers and alerted them to the fact that something unusual was going on. They just didn't know what. And there was certainly a lot going on in the skies above the city as a rescue mission quickly swung into action with choppers being despatched from the likes of Aberdeen and RAF Lossiemouth to the stricken platform with instructions to pick up survivors and to ferry them to Aberdeen Royal Infirmary (ARI), known locally as Forresterhill Hospital, where arrangements were well in hand to receive injured men. Conscious of the fact that the platform had a workforce of well over 200 some 192 beds were made available; sadly less than a third of these was needed.

Although she had been in bed since 9.30 being dog tired after looking after an infant while in an advanced state of

pregnancy, Lorraine just couldn't drop off to sleep. She was convinced that her future offspring was a boy and, judging by his kicking abilities, one that was destined to represent his father's beloved local football team. Eventually just after one in the morning she dozed off only to be awakened by the ringing of the telephone which she chose to ignore. The telephone number that they had been allocated in their new home bore a close resemblance to that utilised by a local taxi company and as consequence it was not unknown for their phone to ring late of an evening and to be confronted by someone clearly inebriated who had dialled the wrong number.
When it rang again a minute later Lorraine simply placed a pillow over her head but eventually gave in when it rang for a third time and cursing under her breath she staggered downstairs and answered only to find herself talking not to some local drunk but her best pal Paula.

Lorraine have you heard the news?
No I have given up watching the news. It's always just so depressing.
I'm not talking about that. I mean the news about Piper Alpha?
What's happened?
There's been a fire. The men are being evacuated.

Lorraine's first reaction was one of excitement. Kenny would be home a week earlier than she had anticipated and perhaps then she could have a day to herself. One spent in her bed.

Lorraine I think it's serious. The rescue helicopters are apparently heading for Forresterhill rather than Dyce so it looks like some of the lads might have been injured. I think you should be there to meet Kenny.
You mean go there NOW?
Yes right now.
Okay but I'll need to get my Mum and Dad to come and babysit.
Will you be okay to drive?
Oh Dad will probably take me.
Do you want me to come along as well? Just for moral support?
Would you Paula? That would be great. But it's the middle of the night.
No problem. I'm up anyway. I'll see you there.

Her parent's phone was answered after only two rings as both her Mum and Dad had heard about the disaster before they had gone to bed and had sat up trying to find out more about what had happened. Within twenty minutes her Dad had picked her up having left her Mum with Alison, who was sleeping soundly and oblivious to what was going on, and they headed straight for the hospital.
By the time they reached there it was after two in the morning and they were astounded by the sheer volume of people milling about. It soon became clear, however, that many of those who had gathered had no association with Piper Alpha. More than 25000 people worked in the offshore oil industry at

the time and many relatives left behind had no idea of the name of the platform or rig that their husband or son worked on, only that he worked in the North Sea, and turned up when they heard of the disaster in the off chance that their loved ones were involved.
The unfortunate ones who had a genuine reason to be concerned were gathered in the hospital's chapel and when Lorraine and her Dad entered they found Paula already waiting for them. She had secured seats that ran down one side of the chapel close to windows that looked directly onto the helipad so that they could see the men when they began disembarking.
The hospital chaplain who proved to be a tower of strength had helped establish a white board on which was marked the approximate time that the next helicopter was expected and it proved remarkably accurate, the first bearing survivors arriving pretty well on time at 3.30 am. People crowded to the windows to watch the men coming off and only then did the extreme nature of the disaster sink home to those waiting as they watched a man fitted with an oxygen mask being carried on a stretcher onto a waiting ambulance and whisked off at speed.
The mood in the chapel which had already been sombre became even more grave as it suddenly dawned on those waiting that their men could be equally badly injured or even.....a possibility they didn't want to contemplate. Lorraine and Paula were, of course, looking out for only two faces and they began to sink into the depths of despair as one helicopter

after another discharged their cargo of humanity without the sight of either familiar face.
But then suddenly there was Steven, hands heavily bandaged but quite able to walk unaided and the girls' mood instantly changed dramatically. If Steven was there then surely Kenny wouldn't be far behind; sadly that wasn't the case and Lorraine couldn't quite believe it as it became clear that no one else would be coming off that particular helicopter when it closed its doors and took off to allow the next one to land. At that moment Lorraine slumped back into her chair.

He's gone Paula. I've lost him.
Don't be silly.
You saw Steven. They wouldn't have left the platform without each other.
Lorraine, they didn't work together out there. There's a good chance that they would have been in different areas when the fire broke out and would have been rescued separately. He'll be on the next helicopter, wait and see. And take heart from the fact that Steven doesn't seem to be badly hurt.

But Kenny didn't emerge from the next chopper or the one after that. Eventually eleven helicopters discharged their cargoes of injured and distraught men, sixty three in all, in the early hours of that fateful morning but none of those disembarking was Kenny Mutch. It must have been about an hour after the last of those helicopters had landed that someone noticed that the white board hadn't been updated and

it slowly dawned on the assembled throng that no more aircraft were incoming.
Rumours are strange things. Who starts them and why they do it will invariably be the great unanswered questions but their spread can sometimes be credited to someone's desperate need to cling on to a thread of comfort in distressed times. That was what happened in that citadel of despair that morning. The word began to circulate that a fishing boat had picked up a large number of men from the seas around Piper Alpha and was now sailing towards a safe harbour. Details varied. Some people heard it was eighty men, others ninety, while the point of destination was sometimes Peterhead, sometimes Fraserburgh. The exact facts, however, were mildly irrelevant as the mood in the room instantly lightened only to be deflated like a pricked balloon as it was officially announced that there was no rescue boat and that it was unlikely that there were any more survivors. Sixty three was the current number. Sixty three was all there ever would be although sadly even one of those subsequently succumbed to his terrible injuries.

Following that announcement and the lack of an update on the whiteboard the people who were gathered in the chapel began to drift away. At first Lorraine was reluctant to do so but eventually about six a.m. her Dad persuaded her to go. Despite her sweet nature Lorraine had a steely side to her and throughout the long hours spent at the hospital she had remained in control unlike others who were hysterical with some behaving in a manner reminiscent of Middle Eastern

funerals. But when they got back to her house in Bridge of Don that all changed.
It was the simplest of things that cracked her stoicism. The sight of the old green anorak that Kenny constantly wore hanging up in the hallway. She had continually nagged him to buy a new one but at that moment she would have given anything to see him dressed in it once again and the realisation that she never would broke her and she wept copiously.

Despite the pleadings of her children Jean Mutch had never owned a dog and was totally amazed just how much her life changed when a little four legged creature came into her life. The house had felt so empty when her daughter moved into a home of her own with her new husband but even then she hadn't gone looking for a canine companion.
It had all come about on a Sunday morning at church when members of the congregation were biding a fond farewell to the Matthews family who were about to emigrate to Australia. A friend had asked Wendy Matthews *have you found a new home for your dog?* to which a clearly troubled lady simply replied *afraid not. Looks like she might have to go to the Cat and Dog Home in Aberdeen.* That exchange didn't resonate with Jean at the time but only later when she was sitting alone having her lunch and she mentioned it in passing to Brian when he made his regular weekly telephone call to his mother that afternoon. Worried about his Mum being totally alone he was most encouraging, so much so that as soon as he had hung up Jean was calling Wendy Matthews and by that

evening Jean found herself the owner of a cute two year old Cairn Terrier called Hazel.
Within a week Jean wondered how she had survived without her wee pal and the two of them became a familiar sight around the streets of Peterhead. Mornings followed a regular routine, come rain or shine; a walk west along Maiden Street, then Errol Street, Marischal Street onto Tollbooth Wynd and back home for breakfast for them both. It was just as they were about to turn back onto Maiden Street on the morning of 7th July for the last lap that Jean bumped into Kathleen McDonald who was on her way to her job as a chambermaid in the Waverley Hotel.

Mornin' Jean. Grand day isn't it.
It is that Kathleen. I love these light mornins. Jist a peety we are already past the longest day.
Aye. So we need tae mak' the best o' them while we can.
True.
At wis an' terrible accident last night wisn't it?
Oh aye jist terrible. Right I better get goin' Hazel's remindin' me she hisnae hid her breakfast yet.
Aye see you Jean.

Although she had agreed with Kathleen she had no idea what the 'terrible accident' was but wasn't going to admit to that. Everyone in the town always wanted to be first with every bit of news and Jean was no exception. She assumed that Kathleen had been referring to what was just the latest of the horror crashes on the Peterhead to Fraserburgh road. The seventeen mile stretch of the A90 between the two North East towns had become notorious as young lads with too much cash and, as a consequence, souped up cars tried to beat the speed record between the twin towns often with disastrous and, on occasions, fatal results.

As a result Jean didn't even turn on the television to catch the morning news until she had fed a very excited Hazel and prepared her own bowl of cornflakes and tea and toast. Only then did she sit herself down and switch on the goggle box and realise that the events to which her friend had referred were quite a bit more serious than just a car crash.

Being a compassionate person Jean immediately felt heart sorry for those who had lost loved ones while silently saying a quiet prayer of thanks that she wasn't one of them. Two weeks earlier Kenny had called her with the good news about the future job in a prestigious hotel and at the same time told her that when he did return offshore a week later that it would be with another catering company. She was therefore stunned when she answered the telephone.

Hello Jean. It's Lorraine.

Hello my dear. I've jist bin watchin' the tele. That' an affa disaster isn't it? And to think that if it hid happened a few wiks earlier oor Kenny could have been there.

Jean, Kenny was there.

Whit? He telt me recently that he wis gaen to work for anither catering company.

He did. But it was still on Piper Alpha.

Oh dear. And is he a'right.

I'm afraid not Jean. He's not amongst the survivors.

It took Jean a few moments for the information to sink in before she dropped the telephone handset and collapsed into her favourite armchair. Recognising that her owner was clearly distressed Hazel jumped onto Jean's knee and curled up there, oblivious to the tears that fell onto her wiry coat.

CHAPTER FIFTEEN

On arriving at ARI Steven was instantly treated by waiting doctors who asked him how he came to be rescued, their newsy approach probably adopted to take the patient's mind off of what was happening in the confines of the A. & E. Department. Steven had difficulty recalling the events as much of what had occurred in the previous few hours seemed more like a bad dream than reality. As far as he could recollect he had been taken from the Silver Pit after an underground explosion had disabled that vessel by an FRC and transferred to the *Tharos*, a support ship, and then plucked by a winch onto one of the Sea King helicopters circling above. From there it was full speed ahead to the hospital heliport and a fleet of waiting ambulances and medics.

The initial plan had been to take the men to the Skean Dhu Hotel in Dyce on the outskirts of Aberdeen but when it became clear that the men's injuries were far more severe than had been expected that idea was shelved and the hospital staff got into full swing. Much to his disgust the bandages applied to his hands on the *Silver Pit* had to be removed so his palms could be properly treated and fresh bandages applied. Steven wasn't a particularly squeamish person but he did find something else to distract his attention during that particular procedure.

It soon became clear that the medics were much less concerned with the visible burns he had suffered than by the potential effects of breathing in acrid and very hot smoke which they explained could cause major damage to his lungs. As a result Steven was checked for signs of soot in his nose and mouth and for singed nasal hairs. Although he had undoubtedly inhaled smoke, getting off the platform when he did meant that he had probably saved himself from serious long term health problems.

Steven was then transferred to a waiting hospital bed and, heavily sedated, drifted into a deep if rather troubled sleep.

On the evening of 6th July Martin Grant had arrived feeling totally weary. As a consequence of some of his colleagues off sunning themselves abroad he had been forced to work extra hours in a very busy A. & E. Department and after a light meal he headed for bed shortly after 9.30. Always early to bed Evelyn joined him and both drifted off to sleep within minutes. They slept so soundly that they were quite oblivious to the comings and goings at ARI despite the fact that they lived less than a mile from the facility and he was absolutely shocked when he turned on the television the next morning.

Steven and his parents had never had a fall out; they just drifted apart and despite both living in the West End of Aberdeen saw little of each other. Martin was certainly aware of the fact that Steven had been working offshore but knowing his lad's fickle nature wouldn't have been surprised to discover that he was now off picking oranges in a kibbutz in Israel. In any event there were literally tens of thousands of men working on the platforms and rigs in the North Sea so the

likelihood that Steven would be amongst the 200 on the affected platform was slight to say the least.
And yet a seed of doubt remained in his mind as he recollected a telephone call between Steven and his Mum a few weeks back; it was always Evelyn that instigated the contact, never either of the men. He was sure that his wife had made reference to Steven having moved to another platform and the name Piper Alpha rang a bell. He was tempted to wake her to check but refrained from doing so. What was the point in alarming her when in all probability there was no need to be concerned?
He also comforted himself with the thought that if Steven had been attached to Piper Alpha with the two weeks on, two weeks off shift system there was a fifty/ fifty chance he could currently be onshore. To be on the safe side, however, he decided to give his son a call and was a little disappointed when it went straight to his answering machine although that was hardly surprising as Steven had never been an early riser. When he obtained the same response to another call fifteen minutes later, however, he realised that he couldn't continue with this blinkered approach any longer and he had to do something to put his mind at rest.
Evelyn still hadn't appeared at the breakfast table and he decided to continue with his approach of 'let sleeping wives lie' until he could tell her that there was nothing to be worried about. But what could he do? The easiest thing would be to call the hospital but for purely selfish reasons he refrained from doing so concerned that he would be called into help with what was clearly an emergency. He had been working

eight days straight and had no ambition at all to make that nine.
He tried calling Paula, with whom they remained on friendly terms, but without success and, having run out of other options, reluctantly telephoned the hospital. He was shocked when it was confirmed that Steven was on the list of men caught up in disaster but hugely relieved to discover that he had been rescued and was being cared for in the hospital for what appeared to be relatively minor injuries.
Only then did Martin rouse his wife.

Evelyn darling, Steven's been injured but not seriously.
Injured! How? Don't tell me he's been in a bar fight or something?
Nothing like that. There's been a really serious explosion and fire on the Piper Alpha oil platform. Looks like a lot of men have died but I have confirmation that Steven was rescued and is being treated in ARI.
Treated! What for?
Burns to hands I believe. And, of course they'll no doubt be checking him for smoke inhalation. I'm just heading over there now.
Give me two minutes and I'll go with you.
Two minutes? Really?
Yes this is not a time for worrying about how I look.

When the Grants arrived at the hospital on that forenoon they found a scene of great chaos with huge numbers of people wandering about outside, worried relatives mixing with cameramen and film crews. A host of reporters were also chatting to anyone who would speak to then in the hope to garner some snippet of information that none of their rivals had been able to glean. As he was about to enter the building Martin became aware of people carrying photographs which they showed to each and every person they encountered asking if they had seen a missing relative. Sadly it didn't appear as if anyone had.

When they entered the appropriate ward they found Steven asleep no doubt as result of sedatives he had been given and waited patiently until he began to stir. Only then did Evelyn whisper his name and he opened his eyes to see the welcome sight of his parents.

Oh hi Mum, Dad.
Sorry to wake you son.
I wasn't sleeping. Just pretending in case any of the celebrities turn up and wanted to chat.
Celebrities?
Yeah one of the nurses was telling me that they are all on their way, not missing the chance of a photo op like this. Maggie Thatcher is flying up and apparently Armand Hammer the owner of Occidental is driving up from London in his gold Rolls Royce. And Prince Charles and his missus are expected.
Lady Di is coming?
So I'm told.
Maybe you'll get to chance to meet her.

Aye and shake hands with her.

With a wry smile at the remark Steven lifted up his heavily bandaged hands the sight of which caused his Mother some distress.

Oh Steven, are you in a lot of pain?
None at all. They got me heavily doped. Anyway it's good to see you both.
And we are so relieved to see you. What happened?

As this question was delivered Steven's mood changed but before he could respond his Dad stepped in.

I think we should leave that particular discussion for another day. I was speaking to one of the doctors on the way in and they seem to be pretty happy with you. Hopefully they'll let you out by the weekend.
They better. I'll be driven mad by then. You know what a terrible patient I am. My pal Kenny didn't make it.
So sorry to hear that.
I encouraged him to work on that rig and I promised to look after him. And I failed.
You can hardly blame yourself. From what I have heard it was total chaos on the platform.
Perhaps. Still think it was my fault.

Martin interjected when he realised that further discussion on that particular subject was pointless and no matter what was said they would never convince their son in his present traumatised mood.

I have asked them to let me know when you are getting released so we can arrange to pick you up and your Mum is insistent that you come and stay with us until you get better.
With my hands like this there's basically nothing I can do for myself so I won't argue with you about that.
It will be good to have you home again son.
To be honest I'm looking forward to it. Can I still use my old room?
Of course but it's away at the top of the house and we thought it might be better if we converted one of the rooms on the ground floor for you as you might find it a bit difficult to climb the stairs.
Thanks but if I can manage I would really like to sleep in my old room.

As forecast, all the big names turned up on the day after the disaster and toured the hospital chatting in that condescending way perfected by politicians and members of the Royal Family to anyone they found awake. Having already established a friendship with a particularly sweet and attentive young nurse she agreed to give him early warning of the arrival of any of the dignitaries so that Steven could pretend to be asleep.
By the following day life had moved on, the celebs had gone and the wards became relatively calm and quiet much to Steven's delight. Being heavily sedated he slept for hours at a

time missing visits from a number of friends including Paula who brought him a large tub of Quality Street. Next time he met her he was determined to ask her how she expected him to unwrap chocolates with two heavily bandaged hands. Fortunately one of the kind nurses would unwrap one for him every time she passed and as he lay there getting hand fed chocolates by an attractive young girl he felt like Nero in ancient Rome.

By day three they reduced the level of pain killers and he was desperate to get out of the hospital and to return to something closer to normal life. A day later his wish came true as he was discharged from the hospital and his Dad picked him up and took him to the King's Gate house and his old boyhood bedroom where his mother ran after him morning, noon and night.

A week later after his bandages had been changed he headed back to his own flat although he remained in close contact with his parents, his mother calling him at least once every day. He didn't quite believe it but he began to look forward to her calls as unable or perhaps more accurately unwilling to venture out into the big bad world he suddenly felt very alone and vulnerable. He was therefore delighted when Paula came to visit.

Hi Steven. Don't want to intrude but I was just passing so I thought I would drop in to see how you were.

You're a sight for sore eyes.

I did drop in to see you at the hospital but you were out for the count.

Yes they told me and thanks for the sweets.
So how are you?
I'm okay although I am going stir crazy on my own.
Then why don't you go out and about? You look like you are fit enough.
Yes I'm fine. It's just that I'm not ready to meet people.
Have you not been out at all?
My Dad took me to a couple of funerals but that's it. I thought I'd be at a funeral every day but so many of the bodies haven't been found or identified yet and of course a lot of the lads weren't local so the funerals won't be held here.
But other than the funerals you haven't been anywhere?
No.
Were you in a lot of pain?
A bit but nothing compared with some of the lads. There's one poor guy who has seventy percent burns. Seventy percent! And lots of others are also badly injured. No I've been so lucky. The doctors confirmed that they are sanguine that there is no permanent damage to my lungs from the smoke.
That's great. I spoke to your Mum and she said you had stayed with them for the first week.
Mum and Dad were brilliant. You may have noticed when you saw me in hospital that originally I had these huge bandages that made me look like I was in the film 'The Mummy's Curse'. With my hands like that I couldn't do anything for myself. Imagine being almost thirty and yet having to get your Mother to take you to the toilet.
How are your hands?
A lot better. Just these light bandages now.

Still even with those it must be a bit difficult.
It is. The hospital said that they would send me a nurse to help with dressing and undressing and I was kind of hoping that it might be the one who looked after me in the ward. Susan her name was and she was very nice.
But it wasn't?
No. I answered the door and there stood Nora Batty. I'll tell you it's amazing how quickly I learned how to pull on my own boxer shorts even with bandaged hands
You will really need to get out and about you know? Being cooked up like this can't be good for you.
I agree but I'm scared with my hands bandaged like this that people will recognise me and I really don't want to speak to anyone about what happened.
I'm sure a lot of people must have seen your photo on the front page of the Daily Record.
Aye of all papers it had to be the Daily Ranger. I don't even know how they got that photo. Looks like it was taken when I was leaving the hospital.
'A Hero Survives' was the caption wasn't it?
Aye. A hero! Tell Lorraine that. By the way have you seen her recently?
Aye I was up at her Mum's last night. She's staying with her parents just now.
Good idea. And how is she?
Difficult to tell. She obviously had a weepy stage but seems to be slowly coming out of it.
Well that's something.
She just wants to speak about him all the time.

They were really close. Not like us.

I know. It seems such a shame it happened to them. I think they were the only couple I know who were truly perfect for each other. You really could believe that they would live happily ever after. But I think that having Alison helps. With a toddler who is always on the go to look after means she has less time to sit and mope.

Steven, I appreciate that you won't want to talk about what happened but for Lorraine's sake I need to ask. Have you any idea what became of Kenny?

Not really. The last I saw of him he was heading back to one of the accommodation modules to try and find some of the lads he had been working with that day. I tried to persuade him not to do that but he wouldn't listen.

The thing is Lorraine is terrified that they won't find his body. Kenny used to speak to her about his Grandfather who was lost at sea and how his father was faced with holding a memorial service for him rather than a proper funeral.

I think that Kenny probably died in a cabin in one of the accommodation modules with some of the other catering lads. From what I've been told all the catering staff, all twenty eight of them, are missing and if they hadn't been inside a module I suspect that one of their bodies would have been recovered by now.

So if they were in a module, there must surely be a decent chance that their bodies will be recovered?

I would think so. Only problem is that apparently the modules all collapsed through the damaged base of the platform and are now resting on the sea bed. That said I'm sure they will try to recover them.

At least I can now give Lorraine a bit of hope. Thanks for that.

Mind you I reckon it could take weeks, probably months, to complete that operation.

Still better some hope than none.

By the way, I don't suppose anyone has asked but how are you coping? After all you lost your best pal.

Not too good to be honest. He was even more than just my pal. He was like the brother I never had and I really miss him especially as I promised to look out for him and I failed.

You can't blame yourself.

Really?

All in all it must have been a horrible experience.

Unless you had been there you couldn't begin to appreciate the chaos and madness of that night.

I have read so many newspaper reports based on the testimony of survivors and it sounds like a scene from a horror movie.

You can probably guess how many horror films I have watched and yet I have never witnessed anything like that.

Anyway Steven I better get going. How about you and I going out for a drink next week sometime? Folk will be so busy looking at me that they won't even spot you.

Okay. We'll give it a try.

Right but I'm not going to some of those grotty places you sometimes frequent like The Grill or the Star and Garter.

What about the Dutch Mill?

I was thinking about one of the more trendy wine bars. I'll give you a call to firm up arrangements. I can't wait to tell everyone in the office that I am going out with a Daily Record page one celebrity.
Your workmates must be easy impressed. See you Paula and thanks for dropping by. I really appreciate it.

Steven looked out of the window and watched as Paula returned to her car. For the first time in days he suddenly felt a smidgeon of optimism. Sadly it didn't last long.

CHAPTER SIXTEEN

On the day after the disaster Lorraine's Mum and Dad tried to persuade her to come and stay with them but Lorraine was convinced that it would be a betrayal of Kenny to leave the house that he had given his life for. After two horrendous, sleepless nights, however, Lorraine gave in and moved with Alison, who had no conception of what was going on and just kept asking for her 'Dada', to the family home. It was nice to have help with the little one even if the mood there was as dejected. Billy took the loss of Kenny particularly badly, broken hearted for his daughter but also greatly saddened to have lost a friend.

From the moment that she was born Billy doted on his only daughter and their great affection for each other was cemented by their fortnightly sojourns to see the local football team. But then Lorraine turned into a teenager and like all Dads he began to worry about her as she was faced with the temptations and pitfalls of the modern world. He had never admitted it to anyone, not even Marilyn, but for years he was worried about the day when he would be confronted with her choice of male companion. He was convinced that whoever Lorraine chose as her life partner he wouldn't, in Billy's eyes, be good enough for her. But he was wrong.
From the first time he met Kenny Mutch he liked him. He had a kind, open face and a friendly manner with everyone he met. It also helped that he sported the right football colours but

even more important than that, he was clearly good for Billy's precious daughter. When at their wedding Billy spoke about how he was no longer the most important man in Lorraine's life but yet how he was content to pass that baton to Kenny he meant every word of it.
He had been concerned for the lad when he announced that he was going offshore but at the same time so impressed that he was willing to give up his home comforts and face a life that was clearly alien to him simply to provide a better life for his daughter and their child. Billy was genuinely proud to call Kenny his son-in-law and as consequence devastated by his loss.

But in addition to enjoying the shelter and succour of her original family home there were other reasons that Lorraine was glad to be away from Jesmond Drive. She didn't know how they found her but suddenly reporters began arriving at her door although they were soon dispersed by her ever protective father. The telephone also began to ring with unwelcome calls.
By the time that solicitors offices opened on the morning of the Thursday, less than twelve hours after the first explosion, it became clear that the law profession was potentially looking at a gold mine and even before she moved two days later Lorraine had already fended off approaches for several legal companies wanting to represent her all naturally advising that they had loads of experience and would of course get her the best possible settlement.

Neither Kenny nor Lorraine had ever had any need of the services of a solicitor before they began looking to buy a house of their own. A friend of her Dad recommended a long established company situated on Bon Accord Terrace and they arranged an appointment. As they sat waiting to see one of the partners Lorraine wondered if it would have been more accurate to describe the company as 'ancient' rather than 'long established' and she would not have been surprised if she had encountered Bob Cratchit sitting at a high desk writing with a quill.

The solicitor when he appeared was a man in his fifties with an avuncular appearance and greeted the young couple with a warm welcoming smile, insisting that they call him Stuart. He led them into an office with an enormous desk groaning under the weight of masses and masses of papers that looked like they hadn't been tidied since before the war. Only question was which war? They were offered tea, coffee clearly not being on the menu, and it was served in china cups with milk in a jug and sugar lumps in a bowl along with a plate of bourbon biscuits.

After a brief chit chat they got down to business as Stuart effortlessly guided them through the arrangements to purchase the house and the process of applying for a mortgage. When they left the office they both felt reassured with all of their youthful worries erased. For that reason Lorraine had no doubts whatsoever of whom she should speak about Piper Alpha and its aftermath.

When she was shown into Stuart's office some two weeks after the disaster he immediately hurried to greet her with a bear hug and words of condolence that were clearly sincere and heartfelt.

I'm so sorry lass. I only met Kenny a couple of times but I immediately liked him.
Aye Kenny had that effect on people.
So how are you coping?
Just taking a day at a time. I am fortunate to have such wonderfully supportive parents.
That's good. I take it you've had a few phone calls from the vultures that are circulating?
I had on the first couple of days but I have been staying with Mum and Dad since then.
Good move. Anyway local solicitors have got together as the Piper Alpha Disaster Group because there is strength in numbers and our company is part of it. So if you are happy for us to represent you there is nothing else for you to do. Just leave it with me.
That would be great Stuart. I really appreciate it. I don't want to appear greedy but Kenny was the sole bread winner and as you can see by my condition I won't be able to work for some time.
Lorraine there will be compensation but be warned it might take months although hopefully not years. In the meantime will you manage?
My Mum and Dad have agreed to help out with the mortgage and day to day living costs until I am financially solvent when I can pay them back. I know you can't speculate but will the compensation allow me to pay off our mortgage?

Remind me how much it is?
It was fifty-five thousand but we have paid a wee bit of that back.
Oh my dear I can assure you that there is nothing for you to worry about. There is a format for calculating compensation and a young a man with his working life ahead of him that leaves a wife and potentially two children will be right up there with the highest beneficiaries. I am always reluctant to speculate but I can assure you that it will be six figures and probably many of those.
Really?
Oh yes and while we are chatting can I recommend that once we know the exact amount and the date when it will be paid that you retain the services of a financial advisor? If you like I can give you a couple of names. If you spend some of the money on getting rid of the mortgage and buying a car and probably a decent holiday you should be left with a sum which suitably invested would mean that you could live comfortably without having to think about working. Ever again if you want.
That's so reassuring. Thank you Stuart.
You are welcome my dear. Anything you are worried about just give me call. I am really so pleased that I can help you in some small way.

When Lorraine had left ARI on that fateful day in July she had hoped that it would be a long time before she passed through its doors again. In fact it was less than two months although on the second occasion it was to a rather different part of the hospital in the shape of the Maternity Unit. Her mother had suggested a reversal to their usual roles by insisting on driving Lorraine there, leaving her husband to look after Alison, in case her daughter wanted her in the delivery room with her.

Lorraine initially dismissed the suggestion but when the time came she was glad to have her mother there to hold her hand. Mercifully labour was quick and it was less than two hours after they had arrived when baby Mutch arrived. As Lorraine had suspected he was a strapping boy, weighing in at over nine pounds, and was instantly named Kenneth William Mutch in honour of his father and grandfather. Lorraine had never encountered such extreme and diverse feelings as she did that day. She was ecstatic to be holding a healthy and perfect baby boy while heartbroken that his Dad hadn't been there to witness him entering the world.

She returned to the house on Summerhill Road the following day and once again gave thanks to her wonderful parents who were there to assist her in every way, including the night feeds, twenty four hours a day. The day after she got home Jean Mutch arrived desperate to see her new grandson and bearing gifts including a bundle of baby clothes from her neighbour Mrs. Alexander who was an compulsive knitter. From the very first day she had met her future mother in law Lorraine liked the women and her arrival to see the baby was met by hugs and oceans of tears. It was only then that Lorraine realised that she wasn't the only one who had endured such depths of grief about the loss of Kenny. Now as the mother of a son Lorraine could look differently at how

Jean had suffered. Although he had been in his late twenties Kenny was and would forever be Jean's wee boy.

Fortunately Kenneth was a good baby who was basically sleeping most of the night by the time that he was four weeks old. Lorraine was more than conscious that helping to look after a toddler and a new born was hard work for her mum and dad, neither of whom were in the first flush of youth, and that the time was fast approaching when she would have to stand on her own two feet.

The problem was that she was rather dreading stepping back into her own home with all its memories and kept putting it off by talking about 'another day or two'. But then one morning in early October she made the decision to go for it and informed her parents accordingly. While trying to persuade her to stay on she could sense their relief that they would have their house to themselves again. They did, however, convince her to stay until after the following weekend creating some bogus reason for the proposed delay. The services of Lorraine's brothers Archie and Graham were engaged and the two lads felt desperately sorry for their sister and were keen to help in any way so they could got to work at the house on Jesmond Drive. They gathered and boxed every item belonging to Kenny they could find and moved all the items without Lorraine's knowledge to the loft of their parents house.

They then began work on decorating what had been the spare bedroom converting it into a nursery. With the work complete they helped Lorraine move back to her own house explaining on the way what they had done and that they hadn't thrown out a single item and that she could go through the boxes and decide what to keep at some future date when she was more up to it.

When Lorraine entered the house it felt like a different place and the homecoming proved to be a lot less punishing than she had anticipated. The fact that for some time prior to the accident she had spent half of every month without someone sleeping beside her undoubtedly made things that bit easier although she knew only too well that the road ahead was likely to have its ups and downs. At the same time she felt that she could see a chink of light ahead of her for the first time in months.

CHAPTER SEVENTEEN

When world famous fire fighter Red Adair disembarked at Aberdeen Airport shortly after the disaster it became obvious how seriously Occidental were treating the event. But it soon transpired that Adair and his team were only there to undertake the task of capping the 36 burning wells and the bereaved relatives were far more concerned about if and when the oil giant would begin work to try to recover bodies.

Lorraine, like members of other families who had been unable to organise a funeral, was delighted when she heard at the beginning of August that the first steps were being taken to recover the accommodation modules that were located on the seabed. But then came the unwelcome news that two of the modules couldn't be raised due to safety issues thereby obviously reducing the chances of bodies being located.

It was 11 October before the first module was lifted and sadly for the waiting families it was announced that no one was found in it. Four days later the second of the salvable units was lifted and this time it was discovered that it did hold the bodies of a substantial number of men who had no doubt sheltered there desperately hoping to be rescued.

The next stage was clearly to identify the men and that rather gruesome task was entrusted to a group of twenty officers from Grampian Police who were sent to the Flotta oil terminal on Scapa Flow, Orkney to which the damaged module had been towed.

It took several weeks for the grizzly mission to be completed and throughout that period Lorraine would grab the telephone every time it rang only to be disappointed when it proved to be a friend asking after her or someone trying to sell her double glazing.
But then at the end of October came the call she had been waiting for. The body of Kenneth Mutch had been found and would be returned to Aberdeen for burial within a matter of days. At last Kenny could be laid to rest.

The majority of the funerals of the local victims of Piper Alpha were held at the crematorium but Lorraine didn't want to go down that road finding that place cold and impersonal. With her strong Christian beliefs she wanted the tribute to her husband to be held in a proper church and spoke to the minister of Mannofield Church who knew the Hunter family well and was delighted to officiate at the funeral. A date was set with a private cremation being held later that same day.
Although Lorraine would have been happy for the service to be restricted to a few handpicked family and friends she knew that there were lots of people out there who would want to say farewell to Kenny.

One of those people was obviously Steven Grant and although he knew he would find it difficult he was determined to do his pal justice by speaking out in public about him and what he had meant to him. For the next few days he honed the eulogy he would deliver at the service until he was reasonably satisfied that every word was right and appropriate. He was, however, concerned that it still contained something inappropriate and decided to call Paula and run it past her.

Hi Paula, how are things?
Good. I think.
How is Lorraine coping?
Surprisingly well. I think stoic is the best way to describe her. Her Dad offered to make all the funeral arrangements but she simply wouldn't hear of it. She has been to see the Minister to give him all the information about Kenny that he will need for his address and has booked the Palm Court hotel for the funeral tea.
Busy girl.
I think it has helped to keep her mind off of exactly what is happening. Not sure how she will feel when it's all over.
I finished my eulogy at last. Do you think I could possibly run it past you to hopefully get your seal of approval?
Sorry Steven, what are you talking about?
The tribute to Kenny I want to deliver at the funeral.
Have you spoken to Lorraine about this?
Do you think I should?
Definitely! She has organised this like a military operation and she would not be happy if somebody suddenly decided to stand up and speak. You better call her and discuss it!
Right....
Do I detect an element of hesitancy?
Well it is Lorraine we are talking about.
Do you want me to broach the subject with her?
Would you? That would be great.

I'll be seeing her tonight and I'll mention it and call you back tomorrow. If she agrees you can let me hear what you have in mind then.
Good girl. Thanks. It means a lot to me.

Assuming that it would be little more than a formality Steven gave little or no thought to the subject until Paula, as promised, called back the next day.

I'm sorry Steven. It's a no.
What do you mean no?
Lorraine doesn't want you to speak at the funeral.
But he was my best pal.
Yes I tried to explain that to her but she was adamant. Her Dad is going to say a few words.
Billy! He barely knew Kenny, well not like I did anyway. Is it worth me giving her a call?
Definitely not. You know Lorraine. Once she makes her mind up that's it. You would just inflame things.
Okay, I suppose I have to abide by the black widow's commands.
You will still come?
Paula do you really need to ask? See you tomorrow.
Yes see you at the church. Sorry Steven.
Not your fault and thanks for trying.

When Steven entered the Church the next day he found it was already well filled and nodded towards a few familiar faces from offshore and from haunts like the Stewart Lounge.

Lorraine accompanied by her Mum and Dad and Jean, Kenny's Mum, were the last to arrive and took their places in the reserved seats at the front. As she sat there Lorraine was transported back three years to when she stood beside Kenny and repeated the vow 'til death do us part'. Death had done just that and considerably sooner than she would have anticipated.
The Minister appeared in all his finery and climbed to the pulpit. Having attended nine or ten funerals since the events in July Steven was convinced that there would be a strong sense of déjà vu in the words the Minister spoke. As it turned out, he couldn't have been more wrong.

I had never heard a city cry before but in the days after Piper Alpha Aberdeen wept. It wept for its lost sons and its bereaved daughters. It wept for its lost friends. The cold grey granite facade cracked to reveal a compassionate face as the communal grief brought a torrent of tears. It was then that Aberdeen realised that the prosperity and wealth that oil had brought to the city came at a price. For some, like Kenny Mutch, that price was too high.
We are all mortal. No matter how much money we manage to accrue throughout our lives we all end up the same way and the likes of Bill Gates and Occidental's Dr. Hammer will one day leave the earth as Kenny Mutch has done. All of us here today feel that Kenny was taken from us far too soon but at least we know that he died not to attain great wealth but for a far nobler cause. To ensure a decent standard of life for

Lorraine and Alison and for the little one who will carry on his name.

The rest of the sermon was much more conventional with the Minister recalling anecdotes, some humorous, about Kenny but after it was all over it was those opening words *I had never heard a city cry before but in the days after Piper Alpha Aberdeen wept* that would remain in people's minds. For anyone living in the city through those dark days that phrase perfectly summed up the mood.
After Lorraine's dad nervously delivered a short eulogy to a son-in-law he had clearly liked and admired and the final hymn, appropriately 'For Those in Peril on the Sea', had been sung the crowd dispersed. Lorraine was spared the ordeal of shaking hands with the mourners as they left courtesy of the Minister announcing that anyone wanting to pay respects to Kenny's family was warmly invited to a funeral tea in the Palm Court Hotel.

A substantial number accepted that invitation and the room in the hotel was crowded. Having attended so many such gatherings in recent months Steven was amazed how people would invariably consume such colossal quantities of sandwiches and sausage rolls in a manner that suggested that they had just heard that a famine was imminent.
He was also always surprised at the upbeat mood at such events which was no doubt attributable to escaping from the solemnity and sorrow of the church service and people were clearly ready to smile and even laugh again. Steven sat at a

table with a group of offshore guys, including a couple who had escaped the horrors of Piper Alpha and who, despite the brave faces, were clearly still displaying the mental scars. A wide variety of subjects were discussed but 6th July was never mentioned.

Steven spotted Lorraine sitting at another table looking relieved that the funeral she had craved for so many months, but which she had obviously been dreading, was now a thing of the past. At one point Steven contemplated going over to speak to her but a glance and an almost imperceptible shake of the head by Paula, who had joined the men's table, warned him off.

Some day he needed to have a long chat with Lorraine but clearly today was not that day.

CHAPTER EIGHTEEN

As Paula stepped off the bus at Buchanan Street bus station it felt like she had never been away. Nothing appeared to have changed and it seemed like it was five days, not more than five years, since she had boarded a bus heading north wearing the woollen scarf her Gran had hand knitted for her. It had not been her intention to stay away so long. In fact her final words to her Dad when she left home to go to Aberdeen were *See you at Christmas* and she meant it. But then the chance to work at Ardoe House Hotel over that festive season and the attraction of several days of double time pay coupled with the promise of huge tips was too good to turn down especially in the light of her perilous pecuniary situation at that time.
She had rather dreaded imparting the news to her father but he totally understood, possibly feeling an element of guilt that he had not been able to help to support his daughter financially. Paula had suppressed feelings of guilt by planning to go back home during the summer recess until a fellow waitress from one of the events hosted by the City Council told her all about a job at the prestigious Craigendarroch resort at Ballater. They were looking for staff for the summer season and when Paula learned that she would not only get well paid but would be able to enjoy staying in the staff quarters at the luxury complex she grabbed the chance. It also provided her with the opportunity to see areas of the North East including Royal Deeside. Although her Gran missed seeing her she was thrilled, being a staunch monarchist, to receive a series of

postcards of the area including Balmoral Castle which she proudly displayed on her mantelpiece.
And so a pattern emerged throughout her three years at RGU but one she was determined to break once she began working. She had made plans to return to Castlemilk for Christmas during her first year at Grampian Police until it was delicately explained to her that she was the only member of her department that had no children and that the others would really like to spend Christmas with their kids. She knew it was emotional blackmail but equally she knew she had no option but to succumb to it.

She had begun to wonder if she would ever have gone back but for the events of 6th July 1988 which made her revaluate her life. It wasn't as if she had lost someone in the disaster, Steven having survived much to her relief.
Although they were long divorced that episode had been conducted in a civilised manner with little or no acrimony. Steven had been upset when he learned of her albeit rather brief flirtation with her fellow worker but in truth quite understood how it had materialised. Both of them had realised that they had behaved like a pair of love struck kids and had married in haste and repented in leisure. So for that reason she was truly thankful when she saw her ex step off that helicopter.
She was certainly greatly saddened by the loss of Kenny; after all he was the devoted husband of her dearest friend. More than that she would have to watch Alison, her god child and probably the nearest she would ever have to a daughter of her

own, grow up without her Dad. She was also distressed to see the relatives of all those who had lost their lives on that terrible day not realising until then just how far the ripples of grief could spread.

But the sadness she felt went even deeper than that. She doubted if she would ever forget the words the Minister had spoken at Kenny's funeral *I had never heard a city cry before but in the days after Piper Alpha Aberdeen wept.* She knew exactly what he had meant as she had been there when the city had wept. The city which had become her adopted home. The city that had provided her with an education, with work, with wonderful friends. Before she moved north she was told that Aberdonians were cold and dour but she quickly discovered that that was rubbish. They were certainly reserved unlike the rather garrulous citizens of her home city but soon discovered that once you got to know people in Aberdeen that they were honest and genuine and potentially lifelong friends. And consequently she hated to see the city, where she suspected she would spend the rest of her life, hurting.

But Piper Alpha and its aftermath also made Paula reflect on her own life and the deep seated guilt she felt by the way she had shunned her family and she vowed to do something about it and to go back to see her family to repair fragmented relationships.

She walked the familiar route to St Enoch's before hopping on the number 46 bus. She arrived in a Castlemilk that didn't appear to have changed one iota in the previous five years as if it was the place that time had forgotten. The house next to her family home still had a well furnished garden and she would have sworn that it was in fact the same three piece suite that had been dumped outside on the day when she left. Her Dad was also remarkably unchanged other than being a little more corpulent and he grabbed her in a embrace, reluctant to let go in case she would disappear again. Her mother was in her usual spot, curled up on the settee with an ashtray overflowing with cigarette butts by her side. She barely acknowledged Paula's arrival and she wasn't sure if it was because her mother was having one of her particularly bad days or whether she still hadn't forgiven Paula for leaving home and forcing her back into the work force. While everything up until that moment looked like time had stood still when she looked more closely she could see that her Mother had changed dramatically. She was skeletal and her hair was grey and long and lank making her look like a woman in her seventies and not one that had barely turned fifty.

There was, however, an even more dramatic change in the Webster house. Gone was the tatty and worn moquette suite, replaced by two leather, genuine leather by the looks of them, settees while the living room also boasted what appeared to be an expensive stereo system and the largest television set Paula had ever seen. Clearly mystified by the transformation Paula enquired as to where all the new household items had come from, hoping that they hadn't fallen off the back of a lorry, and was relieved and amazed when her Dad replied *it's all thanks to Alfie.*

When he left school Alfie measured five foot two inches and his Dad worried about how he could find a job. He applied for several including a number of apprenticeships none of which he got. No one would admit it but both Alfie and his Dad were convinced that he was being rejected because of his restricted height but then suddenly due to a quirk of fate Alfie found a job that suited him perfectly.
The Webster's never had any pets, Agnes refusing to give in to the desperate pleading of her kids on the grounds that she was allergic to animal hair while in truth she was only allergic to the extra house work that it might create. Despite that, Alfie had a deep seated love of creatures great and small and liked to pet the horses that pulled the diminishing number of carts that were seen in the streets around Castlemilk. When the large Clydesdale that towed the rag and bone man's cart had a bite at Alfie, for which he received a free balloon in compensation, he wasn't in anyway put off in the slightest and was back clapping any dog or cat that would tolerate him although he did give Dobbin a wide berth thereafter.
Little did he ever envisage that his affection for animals would provide him with a livelihood and a decent one at that? It was his Dad that spotted the advert in the Glasgow Herald from a racing stable in Ayr looking for a stable boy and Alfie applied. When he arrived the owners took one look at the diminutive lad and their eyes lit up, suggesting that instead of just caring for the horses he might like to ride them. Alfie thought all his birthdays had come together and despite the fact that he had never been on a horse the wee lad was gallus and before he left the stables that afternoon he was

confidently trotting around the yard perched atop a very large elegant race horse.

Even though he didn't turn up at her University Graduation ceremony Paula knew that her Dad was proud of her. After all there weren't many, if any, people from their area that could boast that they had a daughter with a BSc. with honours to their name and he did send a congratulatory card. That said, it wasn't Robert Webster's proudest moment as a father. That came one afternoon in the local bookies when he watched, with many of his gambling pals beside him, as *Hickory Grove*, a five-to-one third favourite, romped home by several lengths from its nearest rival. A horse which the TV commentator revealed was being ridden by an Alfie Webster.

That proved to be only the first of a string of successes for the rookie jockey and his son's success had another and more lucrative benefit courtesy of the regular telephone calls with hot tips straight from the horse's, or in this case jockey's, mouth. Suddenly Robert was winning more often than losing especially as he refrained from betting daily and waited for a phone call before dipping into his pocket.

Word of Robert Webster's insider information quickly spread and before long he had quite a following of men who would hold fire until they saw what Robert was favouring before placing their bets. As a consequence the local bookie was increasingly unhappy and eventually he suggested to Robert with just a slight hint of menace that he might like to take his business elsewhere. Robert was happy to do so; he wasn't concerned which bookmaker had to dig deep just as long as the cash ended up with him which, as was displayed by the rather fancy contents of the house, it had continued to do with welcome regularity.

Paula only had the weekend off work and was due to return to Aberdeen on the Monday morning. There was, however, one thing she had to do before she departed and that was to go and see her beloved Gran. She had been well warned by her Dad that she would find the lady much changed as a result of dementia and that she probably wouldn't even recognise her granddaughter. Undaunted Paula headed for the care home in Rutherglen and found it all a rather harrowing experience.
The smell that only seems to emanate from certain care facilities hit her as soon as she opened the door but at least she found her Gran in a light and airy room of her own. She had been old when Paula had last seen her but now she looked positively decrepit. She sat in front of a TV and stared at the screen despite the fact that she had clearly not chosen the channel unless she was secretly studying for an Open University course. Paula held her hand and spoke to her at length but without a single word being uttered by the old lady or even a glance in Paula's direction.
Although she felt bad to leave after only twenty minutes she realised it was a pointless exercise. The grandmother she had spent so much time with was gone, stolen by a cruel disease. She kissed the top of her head and headed for the door but just as she was about to the leave the room a frail voice said *Bye Paula.* Paula was ready to return until she saw that her Gran was back staring at the TV and Paula quietly left the home

with tears running down her cheeks convinced that she would never see that precious lady again.

On the following Monday morning Paula left the family home with her mother giving her a huge hug and whispering an apology for being so distant. Paula new that her mother couldn't do anything about her illness but that didn't make it any less sad. Her Dad travelled with Paula on the bus into the centre of Glasgow and insisted on carrying her bag to the bus station. Before he left for work he asked her if she would think of coming back at Christmas. Paula responded by requesting he set a place for her at the dinner table and this time she know it was no idle promise. Come hell or high water, she would be there.

CHAPTER NINETEEN

During the week after being discharged from hospital Steven was amazed by just how much he had enjoyed spending time with the parents and especially being waited on hand and foot by his mother who had somehow managed to secure a week away from her GP practice for that exact purpose. It proved a unique opportunity to reconnect with them both.

That week and the dramatic event that had created it proved to be an epiphany in Evelyn's life allowing her to face up to the fact that Martin and her had not been good parents, far too preoccupied with each other and their careers than with their only son who clearly had felt isolated. The reality that they had come close to losing their only child made them revalue their lives.

They both accepted that you could only upgrade his Mercedes salon car or her BMW convertible so many times without getting bored and that the law of diminishing returns applied as each new model offered little more of any use or value than the old one.

The same applied to the foreign holidays that had been such a feature of their lives as they discovered that they were happier living simply in a Spanish villa rather than pony trekking in Peru or snorkelling in the Red Sea. Mind you living 'simply' was perhaps a slight misnomer as the villa they regularly rented in the charming mountain town of Mijas just inland of the Costa del Sol boasted four bedrooms, although they only used one as they had always refrained from inviting friends to

invade their privacy, three sun terraces and one large swimming pool.
As the years had gone past they had become bored with the endless dinner parties and although they did host one occasionally they invented a number of spurious excuses for turning down invitations from friends. They both agreed that there was only so much time you could spend discussing new surgical procedures.
The dinner parties were replaced by Friday date nights which concluded with a Port for him, a Drambuie for her. It was during one of those pleasant evenings that a germ of an idea began to take shape in Martin's mind but despite the wine consumed he was, unlike his son, never rash and he decided to check things out thoroughly in the cold and sober light of day before broaching the subject with Evelyn.
While he hadn't reached the official retirement age several of his fellow consultants had gone early and Martin was delighted when he confirmed that he would be able to take his pension now should he wish to do so. It would be reduced but was still a substantial sum they could live on in considerable comfort. With Evelyn a partner in her GP practice he knew there would be no shortage of people ready and able to step into her shoes with considerable financial benefit to her. The first and most important hurdle had been overcome.
Over the course of several years the Grants had regularly rented Villa Alexandra which they loved because of its panoramic view from a hilltop as well as its total privacy and had been disappointed that spring when the rental agency had advised him that the owner had put the villa on the market and

it was no longer available to rent. They had found another property with considerable charm but which they didn't like quite as well. Since several months had passed Martin was convinced that the Villa Alexandra would have been sold and was thrilled when he discovered that it was not only still on the market but that the seller had dropped the price quite substantially.

With all that in place all he had to do was convince Evelyn. He sat her down and explained at length, considerable length, what he had in mind and its advantages and drawbacks. He could have saved his breath as the moment he finished speaking his wife simply responded *when do we leave?* The following day they put down a deposit on their prized villa and instructed their solicitor to put their own home on the market. It sold quickly and months later they closed the door of the house on King's Gate that had been their family home for more than thirty years for the final time with little more than a smidgeon of regret before spending New Year's Day sitting on a sun drenched terrace rather in front of a coal fire.

Piper Alpha had changed Steven's life in many ways, largely negatively, but it did have the effect of mending bridges between him and his parents. The week he had spent after leaving hospital altered everything and he knew that his mother in particular was taken aback by just how different her son had become. All the arrogance and cynicism seemed to have evaporated to leave a rather sad and frightened boy, one she knew was still suffering nightmares although he would never discuss them. On the day that Steven went back to his flat on Queens Road Evelyn invited him to return for lunch the following Sunday and he readily and happily accepted. Steven didn't know what to do with his life after the fateful day although one thing he was sure of was that he would never return to the North Sea. Fortunately the rental agreement on the flat on Queens Road was coming to an end and he subsequently relocated to a small flat just off Market Street. It was hardly the most respectable part of the city but it was inexpensive and in the centre where he felt most at home. Having dismissed offshore work he had little choice but to try to resurrect his only other talent as a DJ. He soon discovered, however, that the time away had not been kind to him and most clubbers didn't want to hear his collection of singles most of which were years out of date. When he had worked as a disc jockey he had bought several records every week to keep up with popular trends but to be able to please the current punters he would have had to acquire dozens and dozens of new discs and he simply couldn't afford to do that. He was able to pick up the occasional wedding gig where the clientele were less discerning but most of the time found himself behind a bar serving drinks

Sunday lunch at his parent's house became a somewhat regular occurrence and they grew closer than they had been for many years, perhaps ever. It was one Sunday while they were tucking into his mother's home made lasagne, one of her specialities, that his father came out with a dramatic announcement.

We're selling the house.
This house? But you love it.
True but the time has come for a change.
You are bit young for downsizing aren't you?
Who said anything about downsizing? We are just moving somewhere a bit different.
Queens Road?
No a little further afield than that. Spain.
Spain?
Yes. You know how we have loved our villa holidays these last few years?
I should. You have shown me enough photographs.
Well the villa that appears in most of these is Villa Alexandra in Mijas which we now own.
Wow that's brilliant.

And Steven meant it. His mother and father had worked hard for decades and he felt the time was right for them to relax and enjoy life while they were still young enough and fit enough to do so.

So when is this all going to happen?
The 'For Sale' signs go up here this week and if all goes to plan we hope to be able to spend Christmas over there.
And once we are settled Steven, Dad and I would like you to come and join us.
Yes I'll certainly come for a holiday.
We were thinking about more than that.
What do you mean?

Come and stay with us. At least for a few months. A total change is what you need after all you have been through.
But what would I do? I can't just lounge about for months.
Use your talents.
You mean I've got some?
The villa is only about six miles from Fuengirola where there are loads of pubs and nightclubs. You could certainly get a bar job and probably work as a DJ. Think about it.
I will. I really will.

True to his promise he did think about it and although initially he regarded it as no more than a pipe dream, six months later he found himself standing outside Malaga airport waiting for his Dad to pick him up. The villa was even more impressive than it had looked in the photos and for the next two weeks Steven did nothing more than sleep late, swim in the heated pool and lounge in the welcome spring sunshine. Although he had not booked a return flight it had been his intention to return home after a few weeks but by then he could see the attractions in staying on. He toured the bars and clubs in Fuengirola as his Dad had suggested and quickly secured a job as DJ and part time barman. From visiting a couple of these establishments at night he discovered that he wouldn't need to provide the patrons with the latest dance sounds and indeed he would have probably have been booed off if he had tried. It seemed to be that as long as you played the likes of *Come on Eileen* or *1999* or anything by Madonna that everyone was happy.

Steven made a flying visit to Aberdeen, gave up his flat and packed his worldly belongings and a selection of this vast record collection, the balance being stored in his car which in turn was parked in a pal's garage, and headed back to Spain.

Although the events of the previous year had undoubtedly aged him, Steven remained a handsome guy especially with his newly acquired sun tan and girls on holiday with their inhibitions having been left at home flocked to him like a moth to a flame. There had been a couple of flings and holiday romances but nothing serious until Astrid walked into the club and into his life. She was the archetypal Swedish girl; tall and blonde and very attractive and he was instantly smitten. She explained that she was spending a gap year in Spain, working in another bar in Fuengirola.

Steven had acquired a cheap scooter so that his Dad didn't have to ferry him to and from work. The problem was that he often didn't finish until two or three in the morning and although the villa was only a few miles away it was up a winding and dangerous road. He quickly tired of making the journey after a boisterous evening and decided to rent a bed sit which he secured at a very modest rental due to the fact that not many people wanted to live above a very noisy nightclub. Steven and Astrid soon became more than just good friends and within weeks he had invited her to give up her rather expensive hotel room and move in with him and she instantly accepted.

Over the course of that summer they became pretty much inseparable and Steven was bewitched by her. While the nightmares had subsided there were moments that he needed comfort and shoulder to cry on and he concluded that there wasn't a nicer shoulder for that purpose than a ravishing Scandinavian blonde. She told him that she would be returning home in September and had it not been for his previous disastrous efforts at matrimony Steven might have been tempted to propose to her. But he decided to simply enjoy their summer together and let fate take care of the future when September came around.

About two weeks prior to Astrid's proposed date of departure she announced that she would be gone for a night as a friend from Stockholm was spending a day in Malaga and she wanted to meet up with her. Steven would have liked to have gone with her but he had work commitments and in any event it was just one night. Except she didn't reappear as arranged the next day. Or the day after. Or the one after that. Concerned that she had possibly had an accident Steven and his father, who had became fairly proficient in the Spanish language, headed for the Police station in Malaga. The officer listened to their story and explained that it was familiar tale. Young girls from a number of countries in Northern Europe would head for the Costa del Sol and find some young man who would provide them with free accommodation so they could save most of the money they earned. The officer who was remarkably sympathetic suggested that Steven might like to check his bank account but Steven dismissed any such suggestion as he knew the girl and she would never steal from him. The Policeman responded with a wry smile that confirmed that he had heard it all before.

While he considered it a waste of time Steven did visit the bank in Fuengirola to discover that his account was somewhat devoid of funds, a statement displaying withdrawals of the maximum amount allowed daily throughout the previous two weeks. When quizzed by his Dad he admitted that he had frequently given Astrid his card to buy groceries or whatever else they needed and yes, she did know his pin number. The sum involved wasn't huge but it was all the money Steven had saved up that summer. But it wasn't the loss of the money that hurt most; it was the loss of a girl he genuinely believed had loved him and the fact that once again he was shown up as a walking catastrophe.

A week later Steven bade farewell to his parents at Malaga airport.

CHAPTER TWENTY

Jean Mutch basically didn't want to go on when she was widowed shortly after her forty-fifth birthday but with three children to bring up she had no choice but to get on with her life. She comforted herself with the thought that her turn to endure such grief was past while her contemporaries would probably suffer similarly sometime in the future. What she had never legislated for was having to go through such pain twice and when she lost Kenny she was close to giving up.

But Jean Mutch was a woman of smeddum and with the support of family and friends she got through it. After all she still had a son and daughter living with her and by the time they did move on she had rebuilt her life.

Brian proved to be the brains of the family and his mother was so proud when he received an award as dux of Peterhead Academy. Brian had always been interested in medicine; he loved to watch T.V. programmes about doctors and hospitals and would happily view operations and other gory medical procedures being performed. Kenny thought his brother was weird as he would have to leave the room if somebody on the tele suffered as much as a noise bleed. It was for that reason that Brian applied to the Scottish Universities famed for their medical courses and was accepted by them all. Much to his mother's delight he rejected Glasgow and Edinburgh and plumped for a place at Aberdeen and while that still meant that there would be one less place at the kitchen table she was happy that her lad was just down the road.

When Brian moved out Jean consoled herself with the knowledge that Shirley, the baby of the family, was still living at home and, having just turned seventeen, was likely to be with her for some time to come. She was therefore more than a little disappointed when Shirley revealed that she was pregnant, a piece of news that Jean somehow omitted to share with her cousin until her daughter's appearance meant that she had no option.
Fortunately the future father was a decent local lad working as a third year apprentice with a local joinery company and the couple quietly married. When baby Shonagh arrived on the scene Jean's life took a change for the better as her daughter was delighted to have a hands-on Grandmother and Jean never tired of spending time with the little one.

In the days after Kenny's death the Mutch home was crowded with family and friends and a few nosey people who just wanted to have a look around but slowly as the time passed most of them began to drift away like *snaw aff a dyke* as Jean would describe it. But one person she could always rely on was the Reverend Robertson who would turn up faithfully every Wednesday morning to check on Jean and always bearing gifts.

Here you go Jean.
Iain I've telt you afore to stop bringin' rowies. I'll soon be like the side o' a hoose.
Never. And I do know you are rather fond of a buttery.

O'er fond if truth be told. Onywiy here's yer tea. Yer nae wantin' a drap o' somethin' stronger in there are you since it's such a cauld day?
Jean are you trying to corrupt me? Thanks but I've got the car so I'll just stick to the Tetleys. So how has your week been?
Oh fine. I was intae Aiberdeen yesterday to see Lorraine and the bairns. The wee ones fair brighten my day.
I'll bet they do.
It's just....I ken Lorraine meant it as a tribute but there's times I wish she hidnae called the baby Kenneth. Every time I say his name it brings back memories o' my loon.
I can understand. In fact that was a subject I have been meaning to discuss with you for some time. The possibility of some sort of tribute in memory of Kenny.
Fit dae you hae in mind?
As I am sure you are aware Peterhead is a rather wealthy small town as a result of the fishing and now the oil.
Oh aye there's nae shortage o' weel aff folk here.
But sadly there are a number who are struggling financially. People who just aren't able to provide clothes and even food for their children as they would want to. Now the church does what it can but we always seem to be raising money to repair the roof or the heating system or the like. But perhaps you could help?
Me? How?
This is just an idea and you can certainly tell me to get lost. What I had in mind was to set up a Kenneth Mutch Memorial Foundation or something along those lines which could raise money for the poorer off.

Raise money how?
Well for a start you are legendary home baker.
I think legendary is a bittie strong!
Not at all. You could hold a sale of your home baking. And I am sure there are a few others who would like to contribute to an event like that. Mrs. Alexander might knit booties and cardigans for kids.
But far would we sell the stuff?
We would happily give you use of the Church Hall on say a Saturday morning. I would also be delighted to contact all the congregation and I think you would be surprised how many would be interested in getting involved. Have a think about it.
Aye. I'll gie it a bit o' thoucht. Meantime let me refill your tea cup and fit aboot another rowie?
No! Well just a half.

The Minister was true to his word and within days Jean was getting offers of help. One person who handmade candles agreed to set up a stall while a talented local artist offered a couple of her paintings for an auction. But that was only the start as a friend came up with the idea of it being a jumble sale as well as a sale of work and before Jean knew it what had been the boys' bedroom was filled with other peoples' discarded goods including quite a number of items which Jean felt sure the owners were rather glad to see the back off.
On the Friday night before the sale Jean and a few friends met in the church hall and set up, ready for the following morning. Jean arrived early on the Saturday morning for no other reason than she couldn't sleep as she was so nervous that the

whole idea would flop. She was convinced that no one would turn up and she would be faced with carting boxes and boxes of goods back to her house.
But then the doors opened and what could only be described as deluge of humanity poured into the hall. Jean was flabbergasted although Reverend Robertson was less surprised pointing out that there wasn't a lot to do in Peterhead on a Saturday morning. By lunchtime when the last of the customers departed most of the stalls were almost devoid of merchandise and the Kenny Mutch Memorial Foundation was suddenly two hundred and twelve pounds thirty pence better off, not counting the selection of foreign coins someone had sneaked in.
If Jean thought that was the end of it then she was gravely mistaken. The word was out that Jean Mutch was on the lookout for jumble and barely a day went by without someone turning up at her house with goods while from time to time she would find items left on her doorstep by people obviously not wishing to be identified.
It was clear that another sale would need to be organised and following its success, which financially exceeded its predecessor, the Reverend Robertson suggested that it would be worthwhile establishing the Foundation as a registered Scottish charity. Jean liked the idea but had no idea how to go about doing that; the ever helpful and supportive Minister explained that he would be willing to do the needful and that providing Jean was agreeable both he and his wife would be happy to act as trustees. Jean was more than happy with such

an arrangement and less than six weeks later OSCR recognised Scotland's latest charity.
Although the money from the sales had begun to make a difference for a number of local families, Jean being particularly pleased to learn that several kids would wake up on Christmas morning to discover that Santa hadn't forgotten them, she had never been one to rest on her laurels and felt that there was more they could do.

Like all small towns Peterhead had a mixture of shops that had been handed down through the generations and others which seemed to pop up and then pop off just as quickly. There was one small shop on Broad Street which regularly changed hands and locals would shake their heads in disbelief at the latest manifestation placing imaginary bets on just how long it would last.
The *Buchan Boutique* had opened in a blaze of publicity in the local press in October no doubt hopeful of catching the lucrative trade over the festive season. Unfortunately the owner, who came from Aberdeen where she apparently ran a successful business under the name of *Aberdeen Apparel,* hadn't done her homework. A stroll around Peterhead would surely have alerted the woman to the fact the town was not a bastion of high fashion and that filling up the rails with an array of anoraks in dull colours would have proved much more lucrative than fancy and expensive dresses and designer wear.
It was therefore of no great surprise to Jean when she passed the shop one day in March and found it was once again vacant

with a 'To Let' sign on display. It gave Jean an idea and one she couldn't wait to run past the Minister when he next came to call. After she had patiently listened to his summary of all the good that the money raised by the Foundation had achieved to date Jean launched into her spiel.

Iain I hiv an idea I wid like to rin past you. Please tell me if I am jist being feel.
Okay but you are seldom if ever foolish.
Dae you ken that shop on the corner o' Broad Street and Rose Street. The ein that is aye seems to be unoccupied.
I think I know the shop you mean. Doesn't it sell rather expensive ladies clothes?
Last wik it did. The day it's lyin' empty.
Again! It hadn't been trading for long.
Less than six month I reckon. Onywiy I ken the mannie that owns the shop and he is lookin' for yet anither tenant. And I windered aboot spikin' tae him aboot it to see if he wid gie us a cheap rent.
Are you looking for somewhere to store goods? I know that your rooms are bursting at the seams.
No, that's nae a problem. This is a big hoose and there jist me and the dog in it. No I wis thinkin' we could maybe open a shoppie.
What kind of shop?
A charity shop.
A what?
A charity shop. There's a couple o' them in Aiberdeen selling ither folks cast offs and they seem tae dae really well.

It might be quite expensive to hire someone to run it.
No. I wid dae it free o' charge. I wid jist need to tae get my sister and a few mair o' the lassies to help me oot and to cover for me if I wis needed for babysitting. So whit dae you think?
I think it's a brilliant idea. If it was a success, which I sure with your driving force it would be, it could greatly increase the money coming into the charity.

Never one to let the grass grow under her feet Jean Mutch arranged an appointment the next morning with the landlord of the empty shop, a second generation Italian who owned a number of properties in the town including its biggest hotel, and poured out her idea to him. He was suitably impressed and offered the shop at half of the rent it had been commanding. And because the previous occupant had paid for a year in advance but only stayed barely half of that time he told Jean that her charity could have it rent free for the first six months. However, that was on one condition; that she didn't tell anyone about his generosity as he didn't want people to know that behind that hard exterior beat a heart of gold.
Having signed the lease Jean Mutch got into top gear and began calling in favours left, right and centre, including the help of Geordie Donald a local painter and decorator who readily agreed to help. And so in a matter of weeks the sign above the door no longer read *Buchan Boutique* but proudly announced that the shop was now the *Kenny Mutch Memorial Foundation* charity shop.

In a place the size of Peterhead where gossip is an important if not the chief currency word quickly spread and Jean was approached by a reporter from the local newspaper the *Buchan Observer* keen on doing an article as well as sending a photographer to the official opening. But he was far from alone in expressing interest as the *Press and Journal* also attended and even a film crew from Grampian Television turned up on the day.

Despite being normally a shy and retiring person Jean Mutch stood there proudly posing for photographs and answering a host of questions from the assembled media. Proudly because she was in her mind speaking on behalf of her son.

CHAPTER TWENTY ONE

After he returned from Spain Steven reverted to a routine that was rather similar to his late teenage years. Sleeping until lunchtime, lounging about all afternoon watching his collection of videos while avoiding, for obvious reasons, disaster movies, consuming a carry out pizza and then an early night. From time to time to alleviate the boredom he would go out for a pint or two but the lack of ready cash meant that intense drinking sessions were a thing of the past.
He had hoped to return from his summer in Mijas with enough money to see him through the winter but the Swedish siren had put paid to that. To no one's surprise Astrid, if that was even her real name, was never found although he greatly doubted that the Spanish police had tried too hard. He knew that Piper Alpha compensation money would be forthcoming but equally was well aware that it could be some time off before it actually materialised.
In the meantime he just had to be sensible with his ever decreasing nest egg and one afternoon in the Dutch Mill he spent an hour nursing a single pint of lager. Trade was slow and with no familiar faces to blether to he sat up at the bar chatting to Harry the head barmen who looked equally bored. Seeing Steven's glass was almost empty he suggested that he might want a refill.

No thanks Harry. I'll stick with this.
Heavy night?

No light pocket.
Oh I see. Dinna tell the boss man but have one on the house.
You're a pal.
Did you see the fitba last night?
Aye pretty dull wasn't it.
Dae you still go to Pittodrie?
From time to time. Truthfully I can't afford to go to every game now.
Reckon you are going to need to find yoursel' a job.
I know. Somehow I just can't motivate myself to do anything.
You used to work in the Holburn Bar didn't you?
Aye. And half a dozen other city centre pubs.
As a DJ?
Sometimes. Most times as a barman.
Did you ken we were looking for bar staff?
No.
Would you be interested?
Aye, I would be. Besides the money it would get me out of my bed and the house which certainly wouldn't be a bad thing.
Do you want me to see what the boss says? He's in the office working on the accounts.
If you don't mind.
Nae at all. It would be nice to have someone with experience and somebody that we ken.

Steven happily supped his free pint while Harry disappeared upstairs returning in less than two minutes.

Right. He wants to know how soon you can start?

Really? Well tomorrow suits me.
Okay when you have finished your pint nip up and see him and he will sort out the paperwork and fill you in on the pay.

Steven had forgotten how much he had enjoyed pub life and it was great to meet up with a lot of familiar faces including a few guys he had known from the rigs without having to worry about not being able to pay for a round of drinks when his turn came. Another attraction of working behind the bar was that it introduced him to a host of young and unattached girls and he began dating again. Sadly most of these potential romances were ended by the females after one night. One of Steven's favourite movies was *The Odd Couple* which has a memorable scene where Walter Matthau has enticed two young women to the apartment he shares with Jack Lemmon. The Matthau character returns from fixing drinks to find both girls in tears and in decidedly unromantic as a consequence of Lemmon showing them photographs of the wife from whom he is unhappily separated and the kids he no longer sees.
In Steven's case the mood was destroyed as he always seemed to get the conversation round to the disaster and the loss of his best friend. After the fourth or fifth girl came up with some excuse for not seeing him again Steven simply gave up and settled for a solitary existence.

True to her word when Christmas 1988 came around Paula was there in the family home and was delighted when she learned that it was to be a family reunion or close to one; Her brother Ernie was once again otherwise detained. She had read of men who set themselves the task of visiting the grounds of every Scottish League football team. It seemed as if Ernie had set himself a similar mission except in his case it was prisons he was 'visiting'.

Carol was there with her new boyfriend and Paula was quite taken aback by him. Being blonde and buxom Carol had always seemed to attract flash guys with an abundance of money but a distinct shortage of class but this one was very different. Rory hailed from Tobermory and was quiet and well spoken. Not only that but he didn't drink or smoke and never seemed to utter an oath of any sort making them all wonder if it wasn't the Moon rather than Mull that he came from.

The icing on the Christmas cake was undoubtedly the appearance of Alfie. He had followed up his initial success as a jockey with a series of winners. His fearless riding style was soon spoken about amongst the racing fraternity and before long he had been lured away to one of the prestigious stables near Newmarket. His career and his bank balance began to prosper and everyone round the Christmas Day dinner table was enthralled by his frequently hilarious stories of his life as a successful jockey.

Alfie had always been a generous soul and he arrived at chez Webster laden down with beautifully wrapped gifts which were clearly expensive if somewhat inappropriate. He gave his Dad a matching set of cuff links and tie pin, gold plated with a horse's head on them, despite the fact that his father had never worn cuff links and only wore a tie if he was attending a funeral. Agnes, who was at the dinner table in body if not totally in mind, was given a gorgeous cashmere

jumper from Harrods and was totally overcome by the thought that her son would consider her worthy of such a gift.
To everyone's amusement he presented Paula with a copy of a book titled 'How to Find a Husband' although he also gave her a beautiful and tasteful pure silk scarf from Louis Vuitton. All in all it was as lovely a Christmas Day as Paula could ever remember and she was a little reluctant to head back north on Boxing Day but had no option as she was due back at work on the 27th.
When she left Glasgow she certainly didn't think that she would be back in little more than two months and for a far less pleasant event, the funeral of her Gran. Not that it was a day of great sadness as for the previous few months the lady had failed to recognise any of the family and had totally stopped speaking. As her Dad, who wore his new tie pin with his sombre black tie, said *it's a blessing she awa'* although he did so with a tear in his eye. After all it was still his Mum.

Paula found the book that Alfie had given her amusing although she had no interest whatsoever in finding a husband; she had tried it once and to her mind once was enough. Not that she lived a Nun like existence but quite the contrary. She was a regular in several night clubs and had a steady stream of male companions. Although she was no great beauty especially when she was viewed alongside her pal Lorraine she was reasonably attractive and kept her hair stylishly cut courtesy of fortnightly visits to a highly regarded hairdressing salon. She liked to refer to her hair colour as light brown and was highly unimpressed when a beau had described it as

'mousey brown'; she didn't regard being compared to a rodent as a compliment and that was the end of that particular not so beautiful friendship.
After the baby arrived Paula and Lorraine met only occasionally and when they did get together they discovered that they had less and less to talk about. When Paula spoke about her latest flame Lorraine looked distracted and Paula was hardly enthralled by the respective merits of Pampers as opposed to Asda's own brand of nappies. In an effort to get her pal back out into the world Paula fixed up a foursome blind date but it proved a disaster with Lorraine later describing the guy she was stuck with as 'sleazy'. It was at that point that Paula realised that in Lorraine's eyes no one would ever measure up to St. Kenny and made no further effort to get involved in Lorraine's love life.

Despite having gone through a divorce Steven and Paula remained good friends and met up once a month for a drink or a coffee. Sometimes friends would stop by their table and it used to amuse Steven to watch their bemused looks when he introduced Paula as his ex-wife. It was while they were having one of the regular meet ups and engaging in small talk that an idea, a slightly strange idea, came to him.

So Paula, any holiday plans this year?
No, I can't afford it I'm afraid. You?
Aye I am heading over to Spain in June for a couple of weeks.
Wonderful!

It is. Living in a luxury villa with a huge swimming pool free of charge. What's not to like?
Sounds great.
It is. Listen, why don't you come with me?
Steven, it may have slipped your mind, but we are divorced.
I know. But the villa has four bedrooms and it's only mum and dad living there so there's plenty of room.
What would your parents think?
They would be fine with it I'm sure. They've always liked you.
Both of them?
Well perhaps dad more than mum but that's to do with mothers and daughters-in-law. It's not a reflection on you. Come on Paula, I could do with the company so that I don't have to speak to the old fogies all the time.
It's tempting I must admit. It would depend on when I could get time off work.
I'm flexible. I haven't booked flights yet and the boss man at the Dutch Mill is pretty good at working round holidays.
Okay, you speak to your parents and if they don't go off the deep end let's try and see if we can make it work.

Evelyn Grant was a little taken aback by Steven's suggestion although once he explained that they would require two separate bedrooms she warmed to the idea. And so in late June the former Mr. And Mrs. Grant headed for Spain. Together.
Paula discovered that the villa was even more luxurious than she had expected and for the first few days she did little but lounge about in the sun. Eventually Steven suggested that he

introduce her to the night life of Fuengirola and two days later Paula was introducing him to another Brit on holiday.
Steven could genuinely say that he had never disliked anyone so quickly and as intensely as Dalton. For a start Steven was convinced the name was made up and that he was probably called Dan or something. In introducing him Paula had said he came from London but the guy quickly corrected her pointing out that he preferred to say that he was from Kensington. Although most people dressed in polo shirts and shorts in the heat of a Spanish summer Dalton favoured a suit, a mohair affair that was so shiny that Steven was convinced that he could use the back of the jacket like a mirror if he wanted to check that his hair was okay. Steven wore a Rolex watch bought with offshore wages but generally didn't like jewellery for men. Paula's new found Kensington chum on the other hand wore a gold bracelet and several rings all topped off with a chunky gold neck chain.
But while Steven couldn't stand being in his company Paula was smitten by him and Steven, knowing from past and personal experience how quickly she could fall under a man's spell, was concerned especially when she began to see him every evening and failed to arrive back at the villa on a couple of occasions.
On the Friday, two days before they were due to return to Aberdeen, Paula announced that she wouldn't bother going out that night as Dalton was meeting up with a few compadres - he had actually used that word – who were over for the weekend for a stag party. As a result she stayed in the villa with Martin and Evelyn while Steven headed into Fuengirola

for a final catch up with some of the people he had befriended the previous year.
Steven and his drinking companions were in one of the popular night spots that evening when he spotted the poser; the mohair suit had gone to be replaced by a shocking pink polo shirt with the compulsory crocodile badge. Dalton wasn't alone although there was no sign of a group of guys on a stag but only a single girl. A very attractive young girl dressed in a crop top and short skirt, both of which looked as if they had been made to fit a Barbie doll, and it soon became clear that Dalton and her were rather more than just good friends.
Steven was left on the horns of a dilemma not knowing whether to tell Paula what he witnessed but on the grounds that they were heading home in two days he concluded that he should keep the information to himself. A discussion with Paula the next afternoon by the pool, however, changed everything.

So have you enjoyed the break Paula?
It's been brilliant. Thanks a lot for inviting me.
So all set for getting back to the daily grind?
Well...perhaps not.
What do you mean?
Dalton has invited me to go and stay with him.
Where?
In London.
Kensington, darling, Kensington.
Yes in his Kensington pad.

Pad? You're even beginning to sound like him. You're surely not seriously considering it.
I am. I mean what have I got to leave behind?
Other than a great job you enjoy with people who respect you and a nice flat in a city you say you love and a lot of good and decent friends. That's all.
I know you don't like him.
No that's not true. I hate him. He's a sleaze bag pure and simple. In fact if there was a league of sleaze bags he would be right there at the very top.
That's not fair.
Yes it is. Paula, it's only a holiday romance and they never last.
You proved that with.... what was her name again? Astrid? You were almost ready to move to Sweden weren't you?
That was entirely different. Our relationship was built up over the course of several months and she was a much nicer person.
Oh yes, as thieves go she was one of the nicer ones.
The fact I went through that experience makes me equipped to see the pitfalls and to advise you.
You can advise all you like but I am seriously considering it. He says he is crazy about me.
And you believe him?
I do.

Steven sat quietly staring into the blue clear waters of the pool considering whether or not he should play his trump card.

Look Paula, I didn't want to tell you this but I can't stand idly by and watch you throw everything away for this guy. I saw him last night.
Yes he was out with his pals who were here for the weekend.
No he wasn't. He was out in the town but it was with a very young girl.
Maybe it was his daughter.
Oh she was certainly young enough but the way they were behaving it definitely wasn't his daughter or if it was he is liable to be arrested.
You're just saying this to scare me off.
No I am just saying this because I care for you and don't want to see you hurt. But if you don't believe me go and meet up with him tonight and ask him. You'll know if he's lying; after all you have had enough experience with men.
And it was definitely him?
It was him.

A clearly disillusioned Paula spent time in contemplation before admitting to herself that she had been having minor reservations about him and the proposed move but had kept them buried.

Right, I think I will just have a quiet night tonight as we have a plane to catch tomorrow.
Good girl. I will ask Mum to cook for four.
Thanks Steven.
You are most welcome. Paula you really do have the most atrocious taste in men.

True. I married you!

For two months after they returned from Spain Paula saw neither hide nor hair of Steven and she wondered if her antics out there had upset him. She was therefore delighted when, after having spent a weekend with a new boyfriend at his house in Kintore, she stepped off the bus on a Monday morning at Aberdeen Bus Station and spotted Steven in the small coffee shop. With time to spare before she was due at work she joined him.

Hello stranger.
Paula. Good to see you. But what are you doing here at this time on a Monday morning?
Just came back from spending a weekend with a friend in Kintore.
A male friend I assume?
Naturally.
Well rather Kintore than Kensington.
Definitely. Thanks again for saving me from myself.
You're welcome. That's what pals are for.
Are you waiting for a bus?
You really are Sherlock Holmes aren't you?
And you always were a cheeky beggar. Where are you off to?
Aberdeen Airport.
Back to Spain again?
No a little further afield.
Where?
Alaska.

Alaska! Strange place for a holiday.
It's not for a holiday. It's for work.
Steven I hate to break it to you but the gold rush is over.
You're wrong. They've found oil now.
You're not going back onto another platform?
Aye.
You vowed that you never would.
No I said I would never return to the North Sea and I won't. But I think that on a platform was the only place I ever felt truly comfortable, felt truly at home. Isn't that sad?
You surely don't need the cash. You must have got a pay out from Occidental.
I did but don't believe all the huge sums being bandied about in the papers. Those quite rightly went to the relatives of the men that died. Survivors got a lot less. By the time that the compensation came through I had accrued quite a lot of debt and I had my car to pay off and ...well you know that I can be a bit of spend thrift when I have cash to my name.
Oh yes I remember. So how did you land this job?
Just applied for it through one of the American recruitment agencies. The oil company were apparently very impressed by my CV.
Really?
I just hope they never get round to checking it out.
But why Alaska? There's surely offshore work much nearer to home than that.
Oh definitely but Alaska is about as far away from Aberdeen as you can get.

Steven you can run away from your home and your friends but you can't run away from yourself.
I can but try.
What happened to that happy sunny guy I spent a fortnight with recently?
He came back here and found reality.
I can only hope you find peace.
Thanks. Right here's my bus. I better be off.
Keep in touch.
Will do. I'll send you a postcard although it probably will only be of an iceberg.

Paula watched as Steven trudged towards the Airport bus with his kit bag slung over his shoulder and she doubted if she had ever witnessed a sadder sight.

CHAPTER TWENTY TWO

Lorraine regularly read of on-going discussions between Occidental's lawyers and those representing the bereaved families and survivors but an agreement on compensation never seemed to be getting any closer. Lorraine wasn't a greedy person but was becoming increasingly embarrassed about living off her parents who weren't only supporting her with day to day living costs but also paying the monthly mortgage.
At one stage she had briefly, very briefly, considered selling the house and moving into a more affordable rented property but she couldn't do it. The house was what had encouraged Kenny to go offshore and had subsequently cost him his life and to sell it would be a betrayal of her late husband. She also contemplated getting a job but couldn't really ask her Mum and Dad to look after a toddler and a baby.
She was therefore thrilled when she got a phone call from her solicitor saying that he had some good news for her and could she come into the office for a meeting. Could she? She would have been there later that same day if Stuart had been free. It was in fact three days, three long days, before a suitable appointment could be arranged.

Come in Lorraine. It's lovely to see you and looking so well.
And quite a bit thinner than I was the last time I was here.
Of course. How is wee Kenneth?

Flourishing. What could probably be best described as a 'big strapping loon'!
That's good to hear. Anyway as I said on the phone I've got some good news. I've got an offer through the oil company and their insurers and one I think is fair. But, of course, you need to be happy with it.
If you think it's fair than I'll be willing to go along with it.

At that point Stuart handed her a document several pages long with a lot of legal jargon. Lorraine skipped through it pretending to take it all in but basically searching for the important bit; the section with a figure attached. When she saw it she was a little bit disappointed. £78,500 was more money than she had seen in her life but after she had paid off the mortgage on the house and reimbursed her mum and dad she wouldn't be left with much to live on and she would definitely have to find a job sooner rather than later.
But then she looked at the figure again and realised that it had three zeros not two. Only then did it dawn on her that the offer was £785,000 and she suddenly felt light headed.

Stuart that is seven hundred and eighty five thousand pounds isn't it?
Yes. What do you think?
I'm speechless. I will be close to being a millionaire. I will be almost as rich as Madonna.
Possibly agreed Stuart although he wasn't actually sure who Madonna was.
So you are happy to sign the form to accept it?

Give me the pen.
It might take a month or so for the money to arrive.
That's not a problem.
There will be fees to pay although they will be thousands rather than tens of thousands so I think you'll be able to afford them without too much problem. And remember to get the advice of a financial advisor before you start spending too much.
Don't worry. I'm an Aiberdeen lass and as a result gie canny.
Thanks you so much Stuart.
You are so welcome lass. In all my years that I have done this job I doubt if I have ever been more pleased to be able to help someone.

The financial advisor Lorraine chose from the list Stuart had provided proved to be perfect for her needs, understanding her reluctance to speculate with the compensation she had received. She wanted to use her new found wealth to allow her to enjoy a secure but yet relatively modest life style and that's exactly what the arrangements he had set up for her did. She paid off the mortgage and bought herself a car. She had no wish to opt for any of the flash German models and indeed initially she was going to go for a Ford Escort but while she was in the garage she spotted a Ford Capri.
It had always been Kenny's dream to own a Capri and now she could make that dream come true on his behalf. It wasn't new as production of the model had ceased a couple of years earlier but it was immaculate and thanks to one careful lady owner had a very low mileage. When she saw it she instantly

fell in love with it and was driving it home to Jesmond Drive the very next day.

Following the accident the Piper Alpha Outreach Group was set up in conjunction with the Grampian social work department and before long they began printing a newsletter called the Piper Line. Lorraine appreciated their offer of help and support after the disaster but explained that she was fortunate to have a wonderful family and group of friends who would be there to support her and help her through the difficult times.

It was sometime later that Lorraine read in the local press about a move by bereaved families to have a statue erected in memory of the men. A public meeting was called and while she thought it was a wonderful idea and saluted all those who were willing to give of their time she was convinced that getting involved was not for her. Convinced right up until the day of the meeting when suddenly she was drawn like a moth to a flame. It was a decision that changed her life.

Lorraine sat quietly at the back of the hall and listened in awe to the speeches. Not the polished and well rehearsed rhetoric of politicians and oil company executives but the heartfelt words of ordinary decent people who were looking for nothing more than an appropriate memorial to the men who had perished and a place where they could visit and pay homage to them.

As she was listening to one stirring speech after another Lorraine recalled a wall plaque in her parents' house with the words of the Declaration of Arbroath 'it is in truth not for

glory, nor riches, nor honours that we are fighting', words which she considered appropriate to the cause being espoused, and suddenly felt empowered to be involved. Those 167 men had been simply wiped from the face of the earth and there was a real danger that in the history of the North Sea they would quietly be forgotten, become little more than a statistic, as the relentless search for the black gold raged on unabated. Lorraine was convinced that should not be allowed to happen.
At the end of the meeting many of the attendees gathered for a cuppa and a digestive biscuit and she found herself mingling and chatting with people who were clearly equally impassioned. When she was asked if she would like to join the group she surprised herself by enthusiastically agreeing to do so and in truth couldn't wait to play some small part in making it happen. She left that hall a different person viewing the future with a positivity she hadn't felt for a long time. But more than that she left with the cloak of bitterness she had worn for so long having been lifted from her shoulders.
Approaches were made to Occidental to finance a statue but for whatever reason the oil giant refused to do so, concluding that having established a book of remembrance in Aberdeen Art Gallery that was sufficient. Lorraine couldn't believe the company's response. The families had lost so much and yet asked so little but undeterred the bereaved pressed ahead regardless.
Sue Jane Taylor, an artist and sculptor who had graduated from Aberdeen's Gray School of Arts, was particularly keen to be involved having spent a weekend on Piper Alpha in 1984 as part of a project and she was eventually chosen for

the task with a budget of £100,000. Now all that needed to be done was to the raise the money.
In the light of Occidental's reticence to be involved approaches were made to the 28 companies who had lost men in the disaster. Seven of those approached didn't respond while others gave sums of as little as £50. The total received from all such sources amounted to £14,000; on the single day of the disaster the value of oil extracted from Piper Alpha alone was close to two million pounds.
Bob Ballantyne, a remarkable man who survived the disaster and dedicated much of his life thereafter to helping the families of those who perished, came up with the idea of Occidental donating the scrap material of the platform but his suggestion was rejected. Eventually the Scottish Office stepped in with a donation of £40,000 to supplement the monies donated by families and others and work began. When Lorraine received the news that the target had been reached and the memorial would be going ahead she shed a tear. For once it was not borne of sadness but of pride in what they had achieved.

The memorial that was created comprised of the figures of three men dressed in work gear on a plinth of pink granite that reminded Lorraine of the material once quarried in Kenny's native town and with the names of the 167 men lost etched on three sides. Lorraine found it particularly poignant to see the ages of the men which varied from a teenager of only 19 to a mature man of 65. The memorial was in the centre of a serene memorial garden in Aberdeen's Hazlehead Park, with 167 roses donated by Aberdeen City Council planted around it, and was unveiled to the public by the Queen Mother on 6 July 1991, the third anniversary.

On that beautiful sunny summer's day over 1000 people attended the unveiling ceremony and amongst them was Lorraine with her two children. She was aware that they were too young to remember anything about it later in life but when they were old enough to understand she wanted to be able to tell them that they had been there to witness the unveiling of a monument to their brave Daddy.
Once the formal proceedings were over and she was ready to head off home she became conscious of a figure hovering behind her and turned to see a face she hadn't seen for a long time.

Steven?
Oh hello Lorraine.
Surprised to see you here. Last I heard you were working in Alaska.
I still am.
So what are you doing here?
I came back for the unveiling.
All the way from Alaska?
I do come back from time to time and I organised my shifts to make sure I could be here.
It means that much to you?
Aye it does.
So what do you think of the memorial?

I think it is magnificent. When I look at it I don't see three statues, I see the faces of men that I once worked with. Men who sadly can't be here. Anyway how are you doing?
I'm fine.
And I assume this is little Kenneth? Mind you I don't really need to ask as he is spitting image of his Dad. Kenny would have been so proud of him. And Alison is a little version of you. She'll break a few hearts when she is older.
So how is Alaska?
Cold!
Worse than here?
Much. Until you have spent a winter's day on a rig that is sited north of the Arctic Circle you've never felt real cold.
So why do it?
The money's good. That's about it.
And when are you heading back there?
On Monday. Going to meet up with a few old pals before then. In fact a couple of guys who also survived Piper Alpha are going to be joining me in the pub later. Looking forward to a serious drinking session.

Having run out of conversation there was an uncomfortable silence before Steven spoke again.

Now all the dust has settled can I ask you something?
Ask away.
Why wouldn't you let me speak at Kenny's funeral?
Because back then I was so bitter.
Why?

To my mind it was your fault that Kenny was on that platform, your fault that he was killed.

Lorraine he was a big lad. He could make up his own mind.

Steven when he was around you he was nothing more than a little boy and one that would have done anything to please you. If you had asked him to walk across broken glass in his bare feet he would have done it just to please his hero.

You must believe me when I say that I honestly encouraged him to go offshore because he was so desperate to be able to provide that house for you and Alison.

I know and I've come to terms with what happened. Back at the time of the funeral I was convinced that I would never be able to forgive you but now I can.

Thanks Lorraine. That means a lot. Now I just have to forgive myself. Anyway I better be off and not keep my drinking pals waiting. Look after yourself. You are such a lovely family and I know Kenny would have been so proud of you all.

As Steven walked away Lorraine had one last look at the memorial which appeared to glow in the summer sunshine. She no longer saw three roustabouts but three images of her husband. Kenny the faithful best friend. Kenny the loving father. Kenny the devoted husband. And for the first time in three years she felt that the sense of pride almost outweighed the sense of loss. Almost.

EPILOGUE

Two years after the compensation money had come through Lorraine discovered that thanks to careful investment the capital sum had steadily increased. While she remained in the semi on Jesmond Drive her Dad would drop hints from time to time about her possibly moving up market to a bigger house in a more fashionable part of town. Clearly she could afford to do so but in truth she had no wish to relocate. The Bridge of Don house had been her and Kenny's dream home and her husband had even carried her over the threshold into it on their first day. The three bedrooms meant that Alison and Kenneth could have one each and with good and supportive neighbours why would she want to stay anywhere else? One thing she did change, however, was the car opting for a top of the range and brand new Mercedes convertible which garnered a lot of very jealous glances as she drove about town.

The invested funds had allowed her to enjoy a very comfortable lifestyle without any thought of having to go out to work. She was a stay-at-home mother to her kids and happy to be just that. Annually the three of them together with her Mum and Dad would head for a fortnight in the sun, always to Majorca and usually to the same hotel, and from time to time would enjoy a weekend break away. A trip to Disney World in Florida was on the agenda but she intended leaving that until the kids were old enough to fully enjoy it.

The only real extravagance that she indulged in centred round Alison's education. As she approached five Lorraine had to get her enrolled at a school and Glashieburn Primary, a two minute walk from her house, had a decent reputation. And yet she had this great desire to see her little girl get the best possible education that the money that Kenny had provided for them from beyond the grave could provide. She also remembered back to when she was small and was jealous of one of the girls from her street who went away every day in the navy blazer of St. Margaret's School for Girls.
She spoke to Alison about it and having visited that scholastic establishment on an open day applied for and was granted a place for Alison in their first year. Alison was a very attractive girl who took after her mother with her long blond hair and she looked amazing dressed up in her pristine uniform and Lorraine only wished that someone special had been there to see it. Several of the neighbours were less impressed and Lorraine and her daughter were the talk of the street for several weeks until something better to gossip about came along.
It had initially been Lorraine's intention to put Kenneth to Robert Gordon's when he came of age but the lad who had inherited his father's stubbornness made it abundantly clear that he was going to the local school and nowhere else. She couldn't believe that she was getting engaged in an argument with a five year old but it was clear that Kenneth felt so strongly about it that she reluctantly gave in. While Alison was a home bird whose best pal was her Mum Kenneth was always to be found in the middle of a bunch kids involved in

all the mischief that went on in the neighbourhood and he was determined that he was going to school with his local pals.
Being an attractive young widow who was clearly 'not short of a bob or two' she didn't lack male attention and turned down approaches for eligible and, on occasions ineligible, men with great regularity. She had found her life partner and the fact that he hadn't been able to be with her along the full length of the matrimonially path was to her mind irrelevant. And so the years passed and all too soon she found both Alison and Kenneth making knowing faces to their mother when she proposed that they better write their letters to Santa. That was a sad day for her not only because it displayed that her kids were growing up quicker than she would have wanted but also because it somehow tarnished the magic of Christmas which had always been so precious to her.

The Hunter family loved Christmas. Lorraine's Mum and Dad were never happier than when they had a house full of people and her Mother didn't mind in the slightest being stuck in a steamy kitchen for days on end. Her Dad also became quite famous in the street as the first person to put lights round their house and even in parts of the garden.
Christmas Day itself was always special with all the close family gathered plus a few from the periphery and over the years numbers increased further when the boys and latterly Lorraine would bring along their spouses or partners or even just their latest flames. Lorraine would never forget when Tommy, the first of the brood to marry, suggested one year that they might be spending the special day with his wife's

parents. Her mother didn't say a word, just sniffed and carried on with her food preparations.

That was sufficient and come 25th December Tommy and Julie were duly seated around the table and the subject of having Christmas lunch other than in the Hunter house was never raised again by him or any of the other siblings. The ensemble expanded year on year as grand children arrived from all directions resulting in two tables in different rooms being required and seats adapted and borrowed. Although Lorraine continued to spend Christmas Day in the bosom of her family after Kenny died it never felt quite the same but it was better than sitting at home morosely sharing the day with just the kids who loved the party atmosphere and the presents emanating from so many sources.

But while her attitude towards Christmas changed after she was widowed the same couldn't be said about Hogmanay. She had always disliked it even as a teenager when all her pals got excited about the prospect. She could never understand the attraction of wandering around Aberdeen in the middle of the night when it was usually cold and raining or snowing purely to visit people you didn't know and would probably never meet again. Sitting in strange houses, dead tired, drinking cheap vodka and eating that strange concoction of cake and cheese knowing that all she had to look forward to was a miserable tramp home and the prospect of wakening up the following day feeling totally rotten.

While she had disliked the whole New Year experience, with its chronic Scottish made TV programmes, when she was younger that developed into a total hatred for the festival as she grew older. But the thought of Auld Lang Syning from 1997 into a new year in particular filled her with dread. 1998 would mark the tenth anniversary of Piper Alpha and the media attention that would undoubtedly generate in the process was liable to re-open old wounds.

And so it proved as the BBC prepared a ninety minute radio programme while Ed Punchard, a survivor who had emigrated to Australia where he became a film producer, produced a film about the disaster. And on the fateful day the local Press & Journal published a special full colour supplement while several other newspapers, local and national, commemorated the event.

Paula was, as always, Lorraine's rock in the difficult times and for that reason she not only organised a day off work for 6th July but spoke to Lorraine's Mum who agreed to look after the wee ones and even keep them overnight. Only then did she reveal her plan for a long and liquid lunch for Lorraine and her in the snug surroundings of Ma Cameron's pub on Little Belmont Street.

Lorraine's initial protests were in truth half hearted and instantly ignored by her pal who had a large gin and tonic waiting for her when Lorraine arrived. During a period of small talk where oilfield disasters were never even hinted at, Lorraine became conscious of the fact that Paula glanced towards the entrance door to the pub every time it opened. Eventually she remarked on it.

Are you expecting some one?
Well....yes.

Who?

Steven.

Steven Grant!

Yes.

I thought it was just going to be the two of us. The idea was we were meeting up to take our minds off what happened ten years ago. And then you go and invite him of all folk.

I didn't invite him.

Then who did?

He invited himself.

But how did he know about it?

Well.....

You mentioned it.

The thing is that Steven and I met for a coffee last week. We usually get together when he is home.

I didn't even know he was back in Aberdeen. I think the last time you mentioned him he was in Alaska or Texas or somewhere.

Oh he's worked all over the place. Currently he's on a rig in the Persian Gulf but he comes back here for a month at a time.

But why did you tell him about this?

He asked about you and I stupidly mentioned what I had planned for today. He said that he hadn't seen you for a long time and he'd love to catch up. Are you okay with that?

I suppose so. Why not? What happened is a long time ago now. So what time are you expecting him?

I said 12.30.

Right, time to order a bottle of wine.

I'll get it.
You bet you will. And I suppose you better bring three glasses.

By 1 pm the bottle Lorraine had fetched had already given up more than half of its contents and there was still no sign of Steven.

Well Paula, it doesn't look like he's coming.
No. The one thing you can always rely on with Steven is his unreliability.

The afternoon developed into a mini pub crawl for the two girls followed by a couple of night caps in Paula's flat. Lorraine reluctantly turned down the invitation to stay overnight just in case her Mum arrived with the two little horrors in tow early the next morning. She was, however, hopeful that with no school to go to that her Mum would keep Alison and Kenneth until lunchtime and, feeling more than a little rough, she was horrified when the door bell went before nine o'clock the next day. But it wasn't her Mum and the kids who were on her doorstep but a young police constable, so young that Lorraine thought he would have looked more appropriately dressed in a blue Grammar School uniform rather than the black of Grampian Police.

Good morning Madam. Sorry to disturb you so early. I'm P.C. Donaldson from Grampian Police. Am I speaking to Mrs. Lorraine Mutch?
Yes officer, that's me. What's wrong?

Nothing to concern yourself with Mrs. Mutch. It's about a Mrs. Paula Grant. Do you think we could speak inside?

Having shown the policeman into the living room, which fortunately she had tidied the previous day, she offered him a coffee which he readily accepted. Judging by his demeanour Lorraine gained the impression that he was rather new to the job and somewhat nervous in case he did anything wrong. She returned with two cups of coffee, one of which she gulped down greedily in an effort to ease her hangover, before collapsing into an armchair.

Right officer, what is this all about?
We are just hoping that you can provide us with contact details for Paula Grant.
I would have thought you would have known how to contact her.
Why?
Because she works for Grampian Police.
Really? I didn't know that.
You probably know her as Paula Webster.
That works in the Lab?
Yes that's her. Grant was her married name but she's divorced. Can I ask why you need to contact her?
It's regarding a Mr. Steven Grant whom I assume is her former husband. Would you happen to know him?
Oh yes, I know Steven. Only too well. What sort of trouble has he got himself into now?

There was a pregnant pause as the young P.C. was clearly not a veteran of tendering bad news. Eventually he concluded that the best approach was just to blurt it out.

I'm very sorry to tell you that Mr. Grant was found dead last night.
Dead? Steven?
Sorry. Yes.
But where? And what happened?
He was found in the bedroom of his flat. A neighbour went to complain about the noise from his TV late at night and discovered that the door to his flat was standing open. She went in and found Mr. Grant lying on the bed and she called 999. An ambulance attended but, sadly, they were too late.
So how did he die?
I'm sorry I'm not at liberty to divulge that information.
Come on officer. I'll certainly give you Paula's contact details but I think I deserve to know a little more.
Right, but this didn't come from me. Okay?
Yes, okay.
All I can tell you is that there were several empty bottles of Barbiturate tablets on the bedside table.
Oh no. But why did you think of coming to see me?
A letter was found in his flat. A letter addressed to you.
To me? What did it say?
I definitely can't reveal that. But in due course after an inquest, if there is one, I will bring it to you if I am allowed to.
Do you promise?
Yes I promise I will.

After the officer had left Lorraine sat nursing her coffee not sure what to do. Should she telephone Paula and break the news or leave that to the Police? She was reluctant to take the initiative, not sure just what to say; after all although they were long divorced Steven and Paula had remained friends, good friends, and she knew that Paula would be most upset. But at the same time, Paula was her best friend and perhaps she should learn about it from her rather than the authorities. After considering the pros and cons for five minutes she reached for the phone.

Lorraine agreed to accompany Paula to the Crematorium. Kenny's funeral had been a very sad affair but in some ways it wasn't as tragic as the farewell to Steven, yet another victim of the Piper Alpha disaster albeit ten years on. Lorraine remembered meeting Steven's parents at her own wedding but she hardly recognised them when she shook hands with them after the service. The Spanish sun tan couldn't disguise the desperate grief that was etched on their faces. It seemed like overnight they had turned into a very old couple.

It was several months later that Constable Donaldson kept his word and arrived at Lorraine's door with the letter that Steven had left for her. It had obviously been opened but resealed and Lorraine couldn't bring herself to immediately delve into its contents. She placed it on the kitchen table where it caught her eye day after day for the next two weeks.
Eventually one night she armed herself with a large glass of a ten year old Macallan whisky and sat down in her favourite

armchair and prepared herself to face reading what were in all probability Steven Grant's last ever words. She found that the envelope contained only a single sheet of paper and the letter didn't take long to read for in fact it comprised of only a single word.

Sorry.

The Doric Board (North-East Tradition and Language) was formed in 2019 as the successor to the North-East Scots Language Board, which had been set up at the instigation of Aberdeen University's Elphinstone Institute and the Robert Gordon University.
The main aim of The Doric Board is to promote the wonderful and unique heritage of language, music, ballad, song, story, history and lore indigenous to the North-east corner of Scotland.

The Board members are volunteers, many of whom have spent a lifetime studying and promoting the culture of the North-east and they bring a wealth of diverse talent to the Board. The stated objective of the Board is: "through advocacy, campaigning, education, public programming, funding and sustained research, to enhance linguistic and cultural confidence in the North-East, being a powerful voice for social, and economic, regeneration, and a driver towards a national Scots Language Board. The Board aims to create and support a sustainable, dynamic future for North-East Scots as a vibrant language, increasingly respected across the region in the context of a diverse and open society."

Over recent years the Board has awarded a large number of grants to individuals, groups and organisations throughout the area to assist the

funding of projects which foster the language and culture of the North-east, one of which is the publication of this work.
The Doric Board is delighted to be associated with "I Had Never Heard A City Cry Before", from the pen of Mike Gibb, one of the area's most respected writers.
For further information on the work of the Doric Board go to www.doricboard.com.

Gordon M Hay
Member of The Doric Board

All proceeds from the sale of this book will be donated to the Aberdeen charity Bianca Friends which supports the Bianca animal shelter in Sesimbra that has rescued thousands of stray and abandoned dogs and cats over the course of the last twenty years. Many of the animals have been re-homed in Germany, the Netherlands, Denmark and many other European countries. At the time of writing the shelter has over 400 dogs and 100 cats in their care. For further information contact biancafriends.sco@gmail.com

The local charity also runs a Holiday & Help scheme for anyone interested in enjoying a holiday in beautiful Sesimbra, a fishing village and beach resort just south of Lisbon, combining it with helping out at the shelter. For further information contact Mike Gibb at the above email address.

Tuesday aft

Anantara Plaza